The Other Side of the Pastor's Bed III

By: Kayla André

Kayla Andrè

Acknowledgements

Issa whole series, y'all! We have finally made it to the end of Morray, DJ, Pastor David, and Geneva's story. It's been a long road, but I appreciate all of you sticking with me. These characters really have a mind of their own and wanted their story told. They'll always hold a place in my heart because this series has pushed me to better my craft, and I thank them and my readers for that!

Dedications

This book is for Tajè, Layla, India, and LunaAudry! My children before I have my own. I love all four of you, and I promise you I'm doing this so that you all will never have to go through the struggles that I had to endure. Thank you for loving me without thinking about all of the wrongs I have done in my lifr. I love you girls with all of my heart and you all are truly

perfect in my eyes!

Chapter One

First Lady Morray Elizabeth

As we all stood in my doorway, watching my husband be driven away in the back of the police car. The emotions going through my body had me at a loss because they were everywhere. The real question was, did he really kill her? As much as I hated the woman, she didn't deserve to die. Maybe she did, but my child's father didn't need to be the one to put her out of her misery. My mother was standing on side of me with her face turned up. Already knowing that she was going to say something that I didn't want to hear, I turned on my heels and went up to my room.

It seems like ever since I got involved with David something was always happening. It was like I never got any peace of mind. If there was a way for me to rewind the clock and take everything back, I would. The problem with that was I wouldn't have my child. Best believe I was going to make sure she didn't grow up like the sick mutha'suckas around her. Right now she was sweet and innocent and she was going to stay that way.

The house was freezing and I wanted it to stay that way because it reflected how I felt. Cold to all of the drama and the pain that I now have to endure. Yea, I was going to go get my husband out of jail, but that would be after my nap. My body was exhausted and all I wanted to do was lay in my bed and snuggle with the pillows. Realistically with two opinionated and childish adults inside of my home I should have known a nap wasn't going to happen, but that didn't mean I wasn't going to try.

"Morray so what are you going to do now that your husband is going to jail for murder? You want to come home because I know you can't afford this lifestyle by yourself. Here I am, fifty years old about to have two kids back at my house." My mother barged into my room as soon as I got under the covers of my bed. Like the diva she was, she was making this about her. I eyed her as she sat down on the edge of my bed, slapping her thighs as she spoke. Troy walked in behind her and stood by the door.

Kayla Andrè

The confusing part is that nobody even mentioned leaving to go back with her. As much as I loved my mother, I knew she and I would never be able to share the same roof now that I'm grown and a mom. "Ma, nobody said that I would be moving in with you. I am fine here. Senior is in jail, not divorcing me. We have more than enough money to make sure that Denise and I are fine. You can go back to your house since you seem to want to be alone in it."

Troy was just standing by the door the entire time on his phone, not talking on it, but I guess he was texting or emailing. "I sent a text to his lawyer and he's asking that you have the bail money ready. He's heading over to the place and wants us to meet him there."

Now it didn't take a rocket scientist to see that I didn't want to be bothered. I was in my bed and under my covers. What made them think that I really wanted to leave it. "I will do all of that when I wake up from my nap. I'm sleepy and I have a headache. Momma if you can't take care of Denise, bring her in here, but I'm going to sleep."

There was nothing else for me to say, so I snuggled deeper into my bed and closed my eyes. I could hear my mother huffing under her breath and smacking her thighs like she had something to say, but she didn't come out and say it. Not because she was scared of me, but because she knew her child and she knew I really was stressed out. The mattress eased out since my mother got up. I heard the door close so decided to take off my pants and get comfortable.

"Morray what are you doing?" My eyes popped opened and I saw Troy still standing in the same spot by the door. How was he still in my room? Did he not realized the door was closed, meaning he didn't need to be in here?

"Troy why are you still here? The door is closed and that's hella disrespectful!" Thankfully I hadn't gotten my pants all the way down and I was under my covers so he didn't see anything. "Get out Troy! I need a nap!"

With the lack of sleep I'd been getting from being by Kedra and worrying about my damn marriage, I needed some time to rest before I worried about my husband's freedom. Senior was a grown man, I was sure he was ok where he was. Besides he

knew people in high places, so he says, I'm sure he'll fair out ok.

My mind wasn't even worried about Geneva's death because

knowing her, anyone could have killed her. She had a lot of

enemies. I can't think of one person who was actually fond of her

right now. Before she had Liana she could run to, but after the

revelation of Steven being David's father Liana couldn't be ruled

out as a suspect.

Troy walked over and took a seat on the chair by the

window. Still with his nose touching his phone screen. He tripped

me out when he started texting with one hand and pulled another

phone out of his pocket with the other. I knew damn for sure he

was more than just some deacon. Didn't no deacon need two

phones. My guess would be he was apart of the secrets my

husband was withholding from me.

Sitting up in the bed, I came to terms with the fact that I

wasn't going to be able to rest until I did what this negro asked of

me. "So what do we have to do?" I picked up both Senior's

phone and my own so that I wouldn't leave them behind.

"We first need to go to the bank, but we need to hurry. Then we have to bring the money to the lawyer. After that he'll try and request a bond hearing, but since it's a murder charge it may be a week or so." Troy placed one of his phones back in his pocket and put the other one to his ear. "I have to get this. I'll wait for you in the car."

A damn week! You mean to tell me that I should get out of my bed in order to bring money so that my husband could sit in jail for a week? These people were trippin, but none the less, I did get out of my bed. Senior's phone started to ring, making me rush to get it since I had left it on the nightstand while I went to the closet. When I got to the phone the screen read Bro. Michael Harrison, but before I could pick it up to answer it the person hung up. I damn for sure wasn't about to call back.

My mother side-eyed me when I told her I was leaving, but when I told her I would bring my child with me she quickly changed her attitude. Just what I knew. She did not want me taking Denise away from her so she asked to keep her. I didn't want to bring my child with me anyways,h so I closed the door to her room and left out. Since we were going to be meeting with

people of some kind of importance, I decided to change out of

my around the house attire into something borderline dressy. It

may have been November, but Tampa was not cold at all. So I

sported a pair of black tights, a black v-neck shirt with a blazer,

and a big grey scarf. Since I wore a scarf, I decided that I would

wear some black booties with a five-inch heel.

When I walked up to Troy's Bugatti and got in. I for sure

know that this man was doing something out the box because this

was a one or two million dollar car. Damn for sure wasn't no

deacon pulling up to church in that. "What do you do?" I fastened

my seatbelt and waited for an answer.

"A lot, but look I'm taking you to the bank to get the

money. When they ask you how you want it, say that it doesn't

matter." Troy weaved in and out of lanes really showing me what

the hell this car could do. Cars began to move out the way when

they saw us coming though. I sat in my seat and just prayed to

God this wasn't the way my life ended.

"You never told me what you did."

"I told you I did a lot of things. There really isn't a need for me to explain it all to you because you don't need to know. You gave birth to *The Martin* so you don't have anything to worry yourself about." Troy looked over at me and nodded his head before looking out the side mirror on my side to get over.

Here it went again, another person referring to my child as The Martin. Even though nobody had said it to me in a while, it still made me feel some type of way. "Why y'all call my baby that? Her name is Denise and she just so happens to be a Martin. Y'all making it seem like she's a savior or something." I waited for a few seconds for Troy to reply, but he didn't say anything so I looked over at him and he looked at me, but still he didn't say anything.

He may not have wanted to answer me right now, but I was going to get my answer really soon. I just sat back in my seat and waited for us to arrive at the place. I thought we were going to go to the place where we usually do our banking, but Troy had us somewhere downtown. After a few minutes Troy parallel parked in front of this massive building and got out. I got out of

Kayla Andrè

the car too and went followed him to the door where a man

dressed in a fancy security uniform held the door open for us.

I didn't even know banks like this existed in real life.

There were floor to ceiling windows letting the setting sunset

display as a pretty backdrop. About six or seven light brown

wooden desks were strategically spaced around the large open

room and each of them had a green lamp. On the right side of the

room was a long counter for the bank tellers to help walk ups. In

the far back of the room there was a big silver round safe door

with two big buff security officers standing guard. Hell, this

damn for sure wasn't Capital One. While I was checking out the

room, a man rushed over to Troy dressed in a pen-striped suit.

"Mr. Haynes, what can I do for you?" The white man held

out his hand for Troy to shake it. I looked over at Troy who had

gotten back on his phone, but did shake the man's hand. "Hello,

I'm Donald Williamson." He introduced himself to me after

being rudely disrespected.

Shaking his hand, I observed how he really looked as if he

was honored that Troy was here. "I'm Morray Martin." As soon as the words fell from my lips, the man stood up straight and

became really apologetic for allowing me to just stand there. He

quickly ushered us to his desk and asked if I needed anything to

drink. I wasn't thirsty, but I wanted a minute to talk to Troy so I

asked for a Sprite.

"Why are we here? Senior didn't tell me we had an

account here." I leaned over and whispered in his ear while he

typed on his phone. I took notice of all of the eyes on me. Each

pair seemed to me more intrigued than the last. "And why is

everyone looking at me like that?"

Troy pulled out his other phone and then put the one he

had out already into a pocket. "David has more accounts than you

can imagine. When you all got married he added you to majority

of them. They are looking at you because you're his wife. They

are holding a lot of his money so they are just trying to see who

he's sharing it with. People are nosey." He never once looked up

from his phone, but I didn't respond to him. I just kept looking

around at everyone who was focused on me. After a while I

started smiling at them, making them look away.

Donald returned back with my sprite, on a silver platter with a champagne glass. Once he sat the platter down on his desk, he opened it and poured some into the glass. "So Mrs. Martin, again please excuse me for having you stand there. I hope you won't tell your husband of my disrespect, but I didn't mean anything by it."

He looked from me to Troy. My eyes found their way to Troy who had placed his phone on his lap and had crossed his left leg. "Donald there is no need for David to know about that incident, but please don't t let it happen again." My eyes grew buck as I listened to the way he spoke to this banker. Yea, something was most definitely up with my husband and the secrets he kept.

"Yes Sir, but what can I do for you all today?" Donald sat up in his chair, looking at the both of us. I really didn't know what we were here for. I mean I knew we wanted money, but I didn't know how much so I just took a sip of my drink and looked over at Troy.

Troy glanced over at me before he spoke. "She needs to withdraw one-hundred-thousand dollars from her primary account." Now, I didn't want to act like I wasn't used to anything, but damn this wasn't no little bit of pocket change. That is the cost of a house, and he said it with a straight face. Donald didn't look surprised either. He just jabbing at his keyboard.

"Ok, well after I place it into the system, I will go to the back and get it for you." Paying closer attention, I realized this man was typing on a Mac desktop computer, wearing a Rolex. He was probably used to see withdrawals like this all day.

It didn't take long before Donald stood up from his desk. "Is there a certain way you want the money?"

"No, whichever way you bring it will be fine." I looked over at Troy, making sure I had said it correctly.

As Donald walked towards the back safe, he nodded his head at two bank tellers who didn't have any customers. These ladies ran over to follow him towards the safe door. Watching this made me feel like I was watching a movie because once the guard saw him coming that way, he flashed his ID over a black

screen and the door of the safe slowly slid open,

In about twenty minutes, Donald returned with a black

briefcase. "Here is your money and here is your receipt. Would

you wish to check it?" This was more than what I was used to.

Never even knew that I could withdraw this much money and

now it was being handed to me in a briefcase.

Before Troy could act on my behalf, I started to count the

money myself. Donald pulled out a money counter to help me.

Not surprisingly it was all there. "Thank you Donald." I looked

up at him as I closed the briefcase and locked it with a key that he

had handed me. We all shook hands and Troy and I left out of the

building. "Where are we going now?"

"We're going to the lawyer's office. He's supposed to be

meeting with a judge tonight so he needs the money. I have a

church meeting tonight so do you want to come with me or do

you want me to drop you off?" He turned the corner on damn

near two wheels and sped into a parking garage of where I guess

the office was. It was annoying me that just because he was in a sports car he was really going over the speed limit like he was

above the law. Like he wasn't a Black man in the south.

There was no way I was going to that church right now

because I knew they were going to be wondering where in the

hell Senior was and I was not ready to answer any questions, and

when I did go, before the baby got here, it was like I was thrown

into a position that I wasn't qualified for. Being First Lady of a

Baptist church was no joke. You had to be on point at all times.

You were supposed to be compassionate, and be able to hold

conversations with perfect strangers about my life. That just

wasn't me. I know God wouldn't put more on you that you can

bear, but I was letting Him know I couldn't bear it.

When Troy pulled into the handicap spot near the elevator

I became so confused because neither of us were handicap. This

was illegal and with one legal problem going on in my life, I

didn't need another one over something so damn petty. Right

before I opened my mouth to ask him why in the hell he parked

here, he pulled out a handicap from a hidden compartment.

"Wow aren't you supposed to be a deacon," I let out a laugh and started to shake my head. Senior's phone started ringing so I took

it out of my purse. Again, the screen read *Bro. Michael Harrison*.

This time I was able to pick it up before the other person hung

up. "Hello?" My voice was as sweet as possible just in case it

was somebody important, but the phone hung up. The three beeps

in my ear let me know they hung up.

   "Who was that?" Troy opened his door, but didn't get out.

I shrugged my shoulders and threw the phone back into my

purse; grabbing it and the briefcase before opening the door. "But

to answer your question, I may do some bad things, but that will

never take away from my love for God."

   His words puzzled me because it was such an oxymoron,

but I let him have that. Troy was about twenty years my senior so

I was sure he was stuck in his ways. We got out of the car and

walked all of thirty feet to the elevator. The garage was quite

updated with the freshly painted numbers on the cement wall.

There weren't even old black spots on the ground, but I still

wasn't touching anything.

I felt kind of out of place when we got off the elevator and I saw all the glass walls with the big *Lockland and & Townsend* displayed behind a waterfall. A lady sitting behind the desk stood up as we approached her, but a large Black man with a bald head came from a hallway. He must've been the lawyer because he lit up when he saw the briefcase.

When he came over to greet us, he looked down at my hand, but he wasn't going to get it that easily. I needed to know that my husband was going to be ok. That he was going to be able to come home to my daughter and I within a week. "So what's the status on the bond hearing?" I fixed my purse strap on my shoulder as I waited for my answer. The lawyer looked at Troy as if he was the one who was paying him. "Excuse me, but I'm holding the money. Now my question was what is the status on my husband's bond hearing? He's being held for a crime he didn't commit."

"Well I'm so sorry First Lady Martin, I didn't mean to disrespect you like that." He nodded his head in front of me. I didn't know for sure what my husband had going on with these people, but I was starting to appreciate how they corrected their

actions. "Can you please follow me to my office?" He extended

his hand out towards the hallway in which he came.

His office was in the back corner. So I was guessing he

was a name partner since his office was as big as the entire foyer.

Looking at this plaque on his desk it read *Jameson Townsend*

confirming my thought. With the all black and silver metal decor,

it looked very office-ish. No personal items except for one

picture on his glass desk, but I couldn't see what was on it since

it was facing his seat.

Once we were all seated, Jameson started to speak. I took

a glance at Troy who was back on his phone. "So as you know

First Lady, your husband is being charged with the murder of his

ex-wife, but what there is no body. What they have is a recorded

phone call from a police dispatcher where they claim Geneva is

screaming for her life and begging your husband not to rape her.

By the time the police arrived to the scene it looked as if the body

was dragged out of the house because there was blood

everywhere. They found your husband's finger prints on the

doorknob."

Taking in what he said, I still felt confused because if

there was no body how was he being charged with rape and a

murder? "And they are actually getting a chance to bring this to

court because?"

"Because D.A. Miranda Scott has been having it out for

your husband here lately. She was the one who stopped the

permit for the community school. I don't believe she will win,

but you don't want this to go to trial at all. With all of the

businesses and assets your husband-" I was so deep into what he

was saying, but he was cut off by Troy's obnoxious cough. I

looked over at him thinking he was dying only to find a death

glare on his face as he stared at Jameson who quickly caught on.

"Yes, we don't want this to go to trial because your husband is a

pastor and it's not a good look."

Even with the age difference between all of us in the

room, I knew they were covering something up. "What the hell

was that. What is it that you all are keeping from me? If you all didn't know, I can legally walk away with this money and find

my own lawyer to get my husband out." Both men fell silent as I

looked at both of them and they looked at each other. "So what is

it?"

Jameson sat up in his chair and looked over at Troy until I

cleared my throat. "I'm sorry, but with attorney client privilege I

am not at liberty to say, but that is something you will have to

speak to your husband about. I can also assure you that I am the

best person to get your husband out."

I knew that they were not going to give me the

information I wanted so I figured that it would be best if I just

brought my tail back home with my child before I cut up on the

wrong people. Honestly there was nobody else that I could call

because I didn't know of any lawyers in the state nor did I want

to chance Senior not getting out. "Fine here is the money and

here is the key. I suspect that my husband will be home at the end

of the week." I handed everything over to him and rose out of my

seat.

"Thank you so much First Lady, and I am about to head over to meet with the judge so I can have the hearing go in our favor." He took the briefcase from my hands and rested it on his desk, placing the key on top. Not bothering to check the money.

Throwing my purse over my shoulder, I headed over to the door, but I noticed that Troy wasn't right on my heels so I cleared my throat. "Give me one second Morray." He got up from his chair and looked back at me. Jameson looked over to me as well; I guess they needed alone time.

"Well can I have your keys?" Troy walked over to me and handed me his keys. He closed the door behind me and it made me feel uneasy knowing they were talking about something they didn't want for me to know, but I was turning the wheels in my head to try and see what all my husband could be keeping from me and why was it so big.

He couldn't have been this major drug lord or anything because that just wasn't him, but still I didn't know what it could be. I hated walking back to the car by myself since the sun had set, but I guess I had to walk by faith and not by sight. Just as I got off the elevator my phone rang and it was a 1-800 number.

Already knowing it was my husband I answered and accepted the

call.

"Hey Beautiful," his voice was like normal. I didn't know

what I expected, but to hear him sound as if nothing was wrong

made me feel a little better I guess.

"What's up? How are you holding up?" I played around

with the car keys until I was unable to unlock the doors.

I checked my surroundings before I got into the car just to

make sure there were no serial killers lurking around the corners,

but there weren't a lot of cars in the garage anyways. Once I was

safely in the car I was able to continue the conversation with

Senior although I wasn't too sure what I wanted to even say to

him. Just knowing that there were people that knew his secrets

and he wasn't telling me almost made me wanted him to stay

where he was just for a little longer, but I knew that was the devil

talking.

There was noise on the other end of the phone with Senior

telling somebody that they needed to wait until he was done. "My bad Mo. So what's up with everything? How are you and my

baby? You met up with my lawyer yet?"

"Denise is at home with my mother and actually I am here

at your lawyer's office now with Troy. Matter of fact I am sitting

in the car while your best friend has a private meeting with your

lawyer about something that they don't want to tell me about." I

rolled my eyes like he could see it, but it made me made me feel

a little better. "And how do we just have a hundred grand lying

around? Don't no pastor make that kind of money!"

"Babe I told you I will explain everything in due time.

Right now with me facing this case is not the time baby girl. I

love you Morray, just please don't stress me out with this. What

did the lawyer say about me bail hearing?"

My mood was shot because how in the world can he

actually tell me not to stress him out? As if I'm not the one

running around the city retrieving large sums of money. "David

don't try me right now. Talking about not stressing you when I'm

the one who looks like a damn fool."

"David? Since when have you ever called me David? Since I've met you I've been Senior so please can we not be petty and not go below the belt. Baby look I didn't mean it like that. It's just more than I wish to speak about over the phone. Just give me some time and I promise I'll tell you everything. I love you Baby. I need you and Denise. You not gon' leave me huh?"

His soft tone and sweet words made me toss between picking a fight with a man who was locked up or listen to his words and wait for him to get out. Choosing the latter option, I decided that I didn't want to argue over the phone. I was going to get my answers though, you can cash your check on that.

With Senior asking about me leaving, I didn't know what was going to happen. Not that I wanted to leave my husband because that was the last thing I wanted, but I hated giving definite answers since there was no way to be sure what the future held. "Baby I'm here aren't I?" That was the best thing I could give up.

"Yea you are. So what did Jameson say about the hearing Babe?"

"He said that you should be out by the end of the week."

"That's good, but babe I can't wait to get home so that I could get finish what we started." I thought back to what we had going on before the police came and arrested him in our home, but I wasn't trying to continue any of that right now. Yea, him going down on me was really good and relaxing, but thinking about him keeping secrets dried me up.

The line got quiet because I didn't respond to him. I looked around the garage to see that Troy was getting off of the elevator. His phone was in his hand, but he wasn't on it. Taking a good look at him, he was a nice looking older light-skin man. Almost looked like Laz Alonso. "Troy about to get in the car. You want to speak with him?" Knowing that he was probably going to say no, I started digging through my purse because yet again his phone started ringing and it was the same person calling. "Senior who is Brother Michael Harrison?"

Troy got right up on the car so I unlocked the doors for him, but I kept Senior's phone in my hand and watched it ring. "Somebody from the church I guess, b-but why did you ask?" I noticed how he stuttered on his response. The called ended and I threw the phone back in my bag. Troy started the car and backed out of the parking space. I didn't really want to have this conversation in front of him, but being that he was basically my husband's right hand man, I knew that he already knew everything.

"Because they keep calling your phone. So I was just trying to see why they needed to speak with you that badly, but Troy is about to head over to the church after he drops me off at home. You want me to tell him to relay a message to this Brother Harrison?"

A smile crept across Troy's face. I knew he was listening to what I was saying. "No Baby, but look I have to go. I'll speak with you later ok. Probably call you before bed. I love you and kiss Denise for me. I'll be able to do it myself in a week."

"Yea, I love you too." Not wanting him to say anything else, I hung up the phone. Troy drove down the street, no he sped down the street, but I needed to ask him something. "So is my husband cheating?"

I kept watch as he sat up in his seat and looked back from me to the road several times before he spoke. "No. What? Hell no! Why would you even ask me that?"

Deep down I felt like he was lying because I knew he wouldn't be trying to tell me anything anyways. "Because of this Miranda thing. So are you sure he's not cheating on me? And I'm going home. I'm not going to the church with you."

"As far as I know he's faithful to you, but yea I heard you tell your husband." Troy merged onto the interstate, damn near getting us into an accident. "But he loves you Morray. I know what you may think, but he loves you."

I somewhat believed that he did, but if I found out he was sleeping with someone else love would be out the door.

Chapter Two
Pastor David S. Martin Sr.
Six Months Later

They've had me in this hell hole for six months trying to build a case. I could've been out, but the judge presiding over my bail hearing was still holding a grudge from when I slept with his wife so many years back. Talk about a man being malicious, but since I had been in here my wife had been coming every Monday and bringing Denise with her so that I could see her. I hated for my wife to see me like this, but there was nothing I could do. The church had appointed Troy as the temporary pastor and that was fine by me because it was more of his thing anyway.

Geneva's death had been bothering me because I was supposed to meet with her that night. Matter of fact, I had gone over to some house she was staying in so that we could talk, but when I got there the door was open and there was blood so I decided to leave. I don't think they really believed I did it, but I do believe that Miranda was keeping me in here because I wasn't sleeping with her. Before I even got in here I had saw her at the church and although I didn't mean to sleep with her nor did I

want to cheat on Morray, I guess old habits die hard. Honestly,

the night I laid my hands on Morray, Miranda was the one who

called me to leave. No she wasn't better than Morray, but I

couldn't get enough of it. It was the allure of being able to have

both women.

"Aye Martin, you have company." Marcus, the guard on

duty came to open my cell. "Warden isn't here so you don't need

cuffs. Just walk right in front of me." He stood to the cell once

the gate was fully open. I placed my bible back down on the thin

mattress that was supposed my bed.

In here I wasn't treated too badly. The only thing was that

the warden was so scared to lose his job that he did everything by

the book, and I mean everything. Walking down the halls of this

God forsaken place, some of the prisoners spoke to me. My crew

that I ran with stayed in Block C while I was in Block A. It was

just me and two other men. Both were here for murder as well,

but in their case I know they did it for sure. That didn't bother me though because they had my back in here like I had theirs.

Nobody messed with us, and we didn't mess with anyone else.

Marcus placed me in the room where we met with our

lawyers, but no one was in there. It was just a metal table with

three chairs so I sat down and waited for my lawyer to get here.

Jameson had promised me he was doing everything he could to

get me out, but they kept fighting us. Morray was getting

annoyed with me because I refused to change lawyers. Jameson

and I had history so I didn't want to up and leave his firm when

my family was one of his biggest clients bringing in fifty billable

hours a month.

The door to the room opening knocked me from my

thoughts. "You don't look to happy to see your woman," Miranda

strutted into the meeting room in a tightly fitting skirt and an off-

white blouse that she had tucked in. The sound of her heels

clicking against the cement ground echoed throughout the room.

"Perk up my baby."

"You aren't my woman Miranda, and what do you want?

You can't speak to me without my lawyer present." I made

myself comfortable in this hard chair. I should have known

Miranda had something to do with this when my lawyer wasn't in

here when I got here. She was always trying to get me alone, and

for the life of me I didn't understand why because I hadn't

touched her since I had been in here. Prison was helping me get

my mind back on track and it was helping me get back closer to

God, or so I think.

"Why are you acting like this with me? You want that fat

wife of yours?"

"Miranda, speak of my beautiful wife one more time and I

promise you I'll ring your neck," I watched her as she walked

around the room with her arms behind her back. Miranda was

fine, I'm not lying. She really was built like a video vixen, but

none of it was hers. Yea she was a DA, but she got here by being

on her knees. She was a darn good lawyer, but a hell of a freak.

After she strolled around the room once more, she sat

down in the chair across from me and opened a folder that she'd

brought in with her. "And is that what you told your ex wife? Did

you ring her neck to or did you break it?"

Kayla Andrè

She knew that I was innocent, but of course she was looking for a reason to keep me here, and away from my wife. "Stop it Miranda. I already told you I was home that night. Why are you doing this really? What is your reason for being so spiteful?"

"Because I know you did this. You got rid of her so that you could be with that young girl. Maybe I should be getting you on molestation charges because obviously you like touching little girls." She flipped through some legal documents and then came across some photos of what I knew to be the crime scene. I'd seen those pictures so many times that I could tell you how they looked from memory.

A trail of blood that was only about three feet long and one single hand print on the gray walls. That was all. They said I was caught because my handprint was on the door, but I never disputed that it wasn't. I knew that I had pushed the door open, but when I did see that little trail of blood, I left and went my behind back home.

Miranda took the picture out of the folder and then placed it down on the table before sliding it over to me, all dramatic. "I didn't do it. You are holding me on charges that you yourself know that I did not commit. Tell me what I need to do to get out of here." I pushed the picture back towards her and rested my elbows on the table.

Licking her lips, she put the photo back in the folder and looked at me. "You know what I need David. Just give it to me, and all of this can go away." There were no cameras in here so she was free to do what she wanted, and with her being who she was and me not being considered dangerous because I hadn't caused any problems in six months, the guard who was supposed to be watching the door probably went on a break. I knew she going to take full advantage. "David, you know you miss me. I've made the warden deny all conjugal visits so I know you're lonely."

She stood up from her seat and came stood behind me, running her hands down my chest. I'm not going to lie to you, it felt good to be touched. Once her hands made their way down to my member, it jumped because I wasn't one to use my own hands so I'd been without. She started to stroke it, making it rise straight to attention, relaxing in my chair I figured a hand job wouldn't hurt. I also appreciated resting my head against her large breast. As I was getting closer to my climax, Morray's face popped in my head.

"STOP!" I grabbed her wrists and moved her arms from around me. "I can't do this, I'm married. Just bring me back to my cell." I turned to face her and her pale brown face was now red. I knew she was angry, but she tried to fake it by flashing a smile and throwing her long brown hair over her shoulder.

Miranda stared at me for a few more seconds before she eyed the folder and went to retrieve it. Heading over to the door, she paused and turned back to face me. I knew that she was going to say something slick, but I wasn't going to change my mind. I wanted to be faithful to my wife. "Remember, you are here because you want to be here. Hope you drop the soap." The snarl on her face was funny because she was really hurt over the fact that I didn't want her. "Guard, come get this jackass and bring him to solitary because he tried to fight me."

I watched her as she screamed down the hallway before the door closed behind her. This had been my life for the past few months. I was sent down to the hole whenever I didn't give her what she wanted. Thankfully the guards didn't treat me the way they treated most inmates down there. Although I was shut-off from the other inmates, the guards would come down and talk to me after they made their rounds.

Waiting in my chair for someone to come in and bring me to the hole I said a quick prayer. "God show me a way out. I promise that I will do better." This time I wanted to keep my word to God. With me not doing right by Him, I think that's the reason I'm in this place now.

Marcus came and opened the door to the meeting room, pulling out the handcuffs. "Martin, if you just do what she says you can get out of here. You ain't that much of a Christian if you are in here. Man I would do it. You see that backside on her?" he spoke as he placed me in the cuffs, but my hands were in front of me.

He knew what the deal was with Miranda because he and I would speak from time to time and I told him that Miranda would mess with any man with a hard on, but he'd always just laugh. I was starting to think he was gay because he could've bagged Miranda awhile ago.

"Well you get her then man. I'm telling you to call her now and y'all use this room. That thing gets gushy too. Get at her," I laughed as I turned my head back to look at him as we made our way to my temporary cell for the next twenty-four hours. Just like I knew, Marcus didn't respond. He just shook his head and laughed. He was gay, I'm sure of it.

Chapter Three

David S. Martin Jr.

"Aye, Babe have you seen my charger?" Kia screamed from the bathroom inside of her room. I didn't understand why she was being so loud when I was right here in front of her on the bed, but knowing her it was because she'd probably asked me once before and I didn't hear her.

"Nah, but you had it in my car though." I answered her back, going ham on my game controller, playing *2k*. She smacked her lips and grabbed my keys to go check in the car, but I was still trying to score against the game since I was playing solo.

Since the accident, I'd healed all together. I was a beast on the field and the scouts took notice. Even though they weren't supposed to, the Miami Dolphins were already trying to persuade me to sign with them. I still needed two more seasons before I could officially be placed in the draft, but they were trying to ensure that I was coming straight to their team. Realistically, they

were the better option because I didn't want to leave Florida.

Markia and I had decided to try and work on a

relationship too recently and that was fine by me because I

couldn't be with Kimora anymore and Morray was trying to

remain faithful to my father; not even letting me eat her out for

fun. Kia was a beautiful girl and she proved to be down for me

like I would be for her. The only hiccup in our relationship is that

Hannah showed up on my doorstep here in Miami, telling me she

was pregnant and it was mine.

My phone on the bed beside me started to ring. I wasn't

going to answer, but I saw Morray's name at the top of the

screen. "What's good Morray?" I held the phone up to my ear

with the help of my shoulder.

"Hey DJ. I was wondering what's been up with you? We

haven't spoken much since the death of your mom. You good

because you didn't even have a funeral nor a memorial service

for her. I mean you text me from time to time, but I know this has

to be affecting you." I heard Denise talking in the background.

So, I paused the game and took the phone from my ear so I could

Facetime her. Now that I know that my dad isn't my biological

father, Denise's existence doesn't seem that trying anymore.

"You Facetiming me on purpose?"

"Yea, put Denise on the phone." I waited for her to accept

my call and watched as Denise appeared on the screen.

Baby girl was thick, I mean really thick. Thighs had rolls

on them and her arms were so big. Her beautiful caramel skin

always seemed to be glowing. The only thing was that the baby

didn't have any hair. Her hair was slick and silky, but it lay down

straight on her head. Today her mother had her in this big purple

tutu like always. Morray always had her dressed in something

over the top.

Morray told her to look at the phone. "Hey baby girl.

What you doing with that grape?" Denise looked at the phone

when she heard my voice and reached for it. Her mom and I were

still friends nonetheless, so she did recognize me.

Once she had the phone in her hand, she just stared at the

screen and had thrown the grape down to the floor. "You know my baby be hungry. Tell him Denise. Say don't worry about my

grape."

"You feeding that baby a horse or something because that

child got a double chin coming in." I laughed looking at how an

extra layer of fat appeared every time Denise put her head down.

"Denise you going to talk to me today?" She stared at the phone

for a few seconds before passing the phone back to her mother

making the noise *huh*.

"Don't put that doggone grape in your mouth Denise!

Here is a new one." Morray held a big purple grape in front of

her child who took it and put it in her mouth. At first I thought

she was going to eat it, but then I realized she only had two

bottom teeth being nine months old. Then I watched the little girl

suck all the juice out of the grape before taking it out of her

mouth and passing it back to her mother. "Girl I don't want that.

Too nasty. Give it here."

Morray took the grape from her child and got up from the

floor, I'm guessing to throw both grapes away. "Don't think I forgot about what I called you for. How are you holding up little

boy?"

She knew I didn't want to speak about it. Who would

want to talk about the death of a woman who'd ruined their life.

Although I didn't tell anyone, I didn't even think my mother was

dead. They never found a body and I felt as though she had it in

her to fake her own death. It could have been a kidnapping, but

the DA tried to assure me that there was more than enough

evidence to rule that there was a murder. She also was certain

that my father had done it. That was something that I didn't

question because I knew how they used to get down, but I didn't

tell her that. My mother was an evil spirit so I'm sure she got

what she deserved.

"Morray I don't want to talk about it. I'm fine. I just need

to relax. With the season being over, I've just been trying to get

my weight up and so that I could come back harder next season,

you know." I laid back in the bed, relaxing myself while

watching as Morray walked around in this deep cut orange dress.

Markia walked back into the room with her charger in her hand. She'd always been a little jealous of Morray so I wasn't sure how this was going to go, but I wasn't ready to get off of the phone. "Ok DJ whatever you say."

"Yea, but uhm how is that nigga doing up there?" I laughed at how hard Morray rolled her eyes at the camera before flashing that sexy smile of hers. Markia got in the bed and smacked her lips. Yea, she was definitely going to want to talk about this.

"My husband is fine, but we're trying to see how to get him home. He keeps saying that Jameson is supposed to be doing something, but you know how I feel about that guy. Denise, don't you touch that! I'm going to get your butt." She spoke sternly, pronouncing every word. "DJ let me call you back because I have to meet Helena and Kedra at the church and this girl has gotten my Coke all over her clothes."

Morray hated for Denise to get one ounce of dirt on her clothing or she'd have a fit. "You are going to the church like that?" Her breast were sitting up and out. She knew better than to go to a Baptist church like that. Especially a Baptist church full of Black people.

"It's too much? I need to go change you think?" She looked at herself through the camera, trying to pull up the dress to cover herself, but it wasn't working so I just nodded my head and we both fell out laughing.

"Damn what's so funny?" Kia rolled her eyes, plugging in her phone. "Both of you are just laughing like there was a joke? What's the joke? Let me laugh too."

Since Morray was as petty as she was, she decided to answer back. "We were laughing because of an insider. Something between the two of us. If you were supposed to be laughing, you would've."

"Aye look Morray let me call you back shorty." I hung up the phone before Kia could come back with something that would cause a yelling match.

Morray was never disrespectful to my relationship since I told her I was in one, but that never stopped Kia. If anything, I didn't respect Morray's shell of a marriage. She and I both knew that she didn't love him, but she wouldn't verbally say it since

she wanted to do right by him or whatever she said.

When I hung up the phone, Kia folded her arms and

looked at me. I didn't know why she cared so much because

Morray lived four hours away from here. I laid in bed with Kia

every night, and I let her ride my face. Hell, I thought we were

pretty serious. I hated when a woman was worried about the next

woman. If I wanted to be with someone else, I would have no

problem being with that someone else.

"Man, Kia don't start that bull no. You always do this

when it comes down to Morray. Ain't nothing going on Ma. We

talk as friends. Morray is married and has a child. I'm with you. I

want to be with you." I tossed my phone down on the bed and

picked up my controller so I could finish my game.

Kia shifted her weight around and huffed and puffed,

trying to cause a big fight to break out between us, but I didn't

care for all of that. "Ok, but I know you still love her DJ. Don't

say you don't. You had me thinking she was your baby mama for the longest, but come to find out she was just a teacher you used to have sex with. A damn pedophile."

"Aye look, watch how you speak about her."

"That's my point right there. You are defending her, against me. The person you claim you want to be with. If Morray called you back right now, it would be forget me. I wouldn't even get a text back from you, but you can lay in my bed and talk to this broad on the phone while her nigga is in jail."

Kia was talking about a bunch of things that I didn't care to hear about any of it because she sounded insecure. If she wanted to be with me, she was going to have to grow up. This was why I liked older women. Girl's my age were worried about social media relationships while older women were trying to build a life. So while Kia continued to mellow in her feelings, I was dunking on Steph Curry.

This game was actually helping me get through life. It allowed me to escape the troubles I was facing in my real life. It was like I had nobody to lean on. I shouldn't say I totally alone because somehow my bank account was still being filled every two weeks even though my father was in jail. And even though

he wasn't my father, it was hard to say he wasn't my father

because he was all I knew. He wasn't even a good father. I really

hated him, but I liked him better than Steven because he knew

about me and still turned his back. He knew that I could've been

his, but yet he didn't try to see. I couldn't see myself doing that.

That's why I was trying to be there for Hannah even though she

and I only had sex once. Hell, I used a condom and all, but she

still said she was pregnant so what was I supposed to do?

"Are you even listening to me? Cause you acting like that

game is going to top you off. Why are you doing this to me DJ?"

Knowing that she was going to bother me until we talked,

so I paused the game. Let it be known that I didn't want to pause

the game at all. "Doing what Kia huh? What am I doing to you

because all I see that I'm doing is playing the game and you keep

bothering me with this nonsense."

Maybe I sounded a little harsh, but she was bothering me.

"Nonsense? So it's nonsense that I love you? That I just want us

to work and you be my only? Is it nonsense that I'm scared to lose you? DJ I love you with everything in me. When I got raped

that night, you were there for me. You stood by me and even

tried to go get those fools who did something to me. Ain't

nobody ever rocked with me like that."

Her words were making sense now. I didn't know if I was

in love with her, but I knew I had love for her. I wouldn't try to

hurt her and I didn't want anyone else to. It was just that I didn't

know if I wanted to be with her for the rest of my life. She was

cool right now because we were young and chillin, but this

wasn't a lifetime commitment. I didn't want to make her feel any

worse by saying that since she was already crying. Besides I

knew that she'd be even more hurt when she finds out that I had a

baby on the way.

Pulling her closer to me, I wrapped my arms around her

waist and tried to think of the right words to say. Something that

didn't make me sound like I didn't care. "Baby look I'm here

now. We have to take this one day at a time and who knows what

could come out of it. Honestly, I didn't see a future with you at

first, but you cool. I like you."

I had to have said something wrong because she moved her body away from me. "What the hell you mean you ain't see no future with me? Is it because you so busy worrying about Morray? Sure wasn't worried about not seeing a future with me when you starting forgetting condoms and all. Man get the hell out of my face." She rolled over in the bed and started pulling the covers over her body. Jerking them off of me to put them on her.

She knew that I wasn't trying to be rude or disrespectful, but I was just trying to be honest with her. I wanted her to know where I was at mentally. Hell, we were in a relationship, I should be able to tell her what was on my head. I just looked at her, but when she started talking under her breath, I decided to get up and leave because I was going to end up telling her something that I didn't mean.

"Oh so you're leaving me?" Kia threw back the covers and ran over to me as I walked out to the hallway. "When I tell you I love you and you act like this? Can't even tell me that you love me back. You tell me that you like me. The hell is a like?"

She was standing there, tugging on my arm like a child. She wasn't but so tall anyway. "Kia you are really doing the most right now. I'm just going to eliminate myself from this situation so that way we don't have any more issues." I pulled away my arm from her grasp and headed towards the door. Lloyd and Tiana were sitting on the sofa in the living room.

Knowing that Kia was going to try to get them in our business, I left without speaking to them. For a Friday, it was pretty quiet. Maybe because it was still early and people were at work, but the parking lot was empty. Just a couple of cars. Kia ran out the house with no shoes on her feet, looking ridiculous. She didn't need to do all of this.

While she stood there, just looking at me, I unlocked my car and got in. "Don't come back here anymore DJ, I'm serious. You leave and we are done." She rolled her neck as she spoke. I loved when people threatened me because most times they were hurting themselves more than they were hurting me. So I pressed the start button on my car, and let the engine roar. "Oh you think you're funny. You aren't the only man who wants me. I can get

any man that I want. You know that DJ?'

"Well go get them then. Don't come at me like that

because of me not saying what in the hell you think should come

out of my mouth Markia. You aren't the only female that wants

me. I'm almost damn for sure going to the Pro's, I got a nice car,

I got money, perfect GPA, and not to mention I'm no ugly dude.

I'm talking to you because I want to, but you just reminded me

why I don't talk to young females."

Her face was stuck on stupid, but I was just trying to keep

it real with her. There were women always trying to talk to me,

but she was the one I chose to try and remain faithful to. Again,

this is why I why I only wanted to mess with women of a certain

age. Since the conversation was over, I closed the door to my car

and started to drive off because she was only going to say

something else stupid.

Chapter Four
First Lady Morray

With everything going on, the last thing I wanted to be doing was tearing my damn house apart looking for a marriage certificate. Thankfully my two best friends were here trying to help me. Jameson swore he needed this damn piece of paper to prove that my husband had good character. That was the biggest joke around. My husband was known, no he was notorious for being a cheating pastor. How was proving that he was now married to the woman he cheated with going to help his case in the slightest.

In the back of my mind, I felt like something was off with my husband, His phone calls started coming less and less and his excuse was that he was always being sent to solitary. When I went to visit him the last time he could barely look me in my eyes, but still I tried to keep up the facade that I was so in love. Senior did hold Denise though, but even then he seemed off. Almost like he was keeping something from me.

"You know what I think is stupid? How in the hell don't you know where your marriage certificate is Morray Elizabeth?"

Kedra pulled open a file cabinet with all her might. I thought the thing was going to fall on her.

"Me too because I know where mine is Morray, you should too." Helena chimed in too, but I knew that it was only because they both were bored with this task. Hell, I was bored too, but it had to be done.

Letting them go back and forth a couple more times, I walked over to the bookcase to find the book that would open up his secret room. I felt like now was no better time than to see what in the heck was in that safety box. "Look, y'all keep complaining and it won't be my treat when we go to Dristil's." I eyed them both, causing them to shut up and get back to doing what in the hell they were supposed to be doing in the first place.

Getting to the little blue book, I pulled it back and watched the little shelf pop open. "What in the world?" Helena rushed over to me. "Girl y'all are big time rich. Only people on movies have these. Kedra you see this?" Kedra and Helena both walked into the room before I did. They looked like two kids who just walked into the enchanted forest. Mouths wide open and hands roaming all over the walls.

"Is this a bar? Morray your husband has a bar and he's a pastor? Lord he just keeps surprising me." Kedra laughed as she went to fix herself a drink. I didn't respond to either of them. I was on a mission and to God be the glory because I found the safety box right where I left it.

The box was kind of heavy, I sat down in the chair and placed it on my lap. Of course, I needed a code and the first one that came to mind was Denise's birthday, but that wasn't it. I tried a slew of other dates, but none of them were right. "Girl you are over there thinking hard. Trying to spy huh?"

Kedra had a glass in her hand and I knew the alcohol was already getting to her. Helena had went back in the office leaving Kedra and I alone. "Girl I've tried so many codes and none of them have worked. I've tried Denise's birthday, his birthday, our anniversary, and the code to the safe at the church."

"Try your birthday." She sat on the arm of the chair and watched me as I turned the wheels. On the last number, the safe popped open. "See I told you. Now let me gon check on the kids because Stephenie probably has Denise up there doing all kinds of things and knowing both of my girls they have ordered a movie."

Once Kedra left, I pulled back the top of the box and was surprised that all I saw were random papers and three keys. The first paper was kind of brown and seemed to be old. Another paper had a list of what seemed to be account numbers, and the rest of the papers seemed to be letters. None of the papers were my marriage license. I did start to read the older letter though because it intrigued me.

The more I read, the more I became confused. Whoever had written this spoke in riddles. There were different things about being the head and keeping the family untouchable. The thing that stood out to me the most is the line, *"you get the girl, you will get it all."*

What girl and what did they get was my question. The keys were all brass and I assumed were keys to safety boxes. I kept look at the page of accounts and there had to be at least fifty of them on here. No names to where these accounts were being

held, but that didn't bother me at all. It was just the first letter I

wanted to know about.

"Morray, your cell phone is ringing." Helena's voice

stopped my train of thought. Knowing that it was no one, but my

husband, I rushed to get my phone. I may have been leery of him

right now, but he was still my husband.

I closed the box and put it back under the chair before I

left the room to get my phone. "Hey Babe," I spoke once the

other formalities were out the way. Like asking me if I accepted

the charges.

"Hey Mo. How are you today?" His voice wasn't sweet or

familiar. It was like he was talking to a friend and not the woman

he was bound to. "Where is Denise?"

Leaving out the room to get more privacy, I placed the

phone on speaker and headed to the kitchen. "She's good, but we

are here looking for the marriage certificate. Where did you put

it?"

"It's in the top drawer of the nightstand on my side of the bed. You should know that, but I was just calling to hear your voice. I need to get out of here. I know I have been distant lately, but you just don't understand. With this case and these unruly men in here, I just need you and my daughter. I'ma do what I have to do to get out of here." He sounded discouraged and hopeless. This wasn't the strong man that took charge of everything and walked about like he had all the power resting in his finger tips.

I couldn't really think of the words to say to him besides, "Just get home. I actually miss you." There was a silence between us, but my mind was still talking to me. I wanted to ask him about the letter, but I didn't want him to know I found it at all. Just as I opened my mouth to say something, my husband spoke to me.

"Can I apologize to you?"

"Wait what? What are you talking about?"

"All of this. I should have left you alone, but I needed you." Kedra walked into the kitchen with Denise on her hips and her kids walking behind her. Quickly I took my phone off speaker and placed it up to my ear.

"What do you mean you needed me Senior. I still feel like you are keeping things from me, and I want to believe you, but I don't know. You need to tell me everything starting from the very beginning."

"Baby I can't right now, but one day I will. I love you. I gotta go, but let's pray I get home soon. I'll call you tonight." With that, the line went dead.

Kedra was standing there watching me while her girls made silly faces at my baby who just giggled her chubby little self away. I put the phone down on the island and looked at my cousin and had an unspoken conversation. We both knew that I was stuck because I ran my fingers across my bottom lip.

I want Senior home so that we could talk about this face to face, but that wasn't the case. He was locked up for a murder of his ex-wife, and I was here with a baby. I know my life could be so much worse, but this felt like the lowest point of my life.

Kayla Andrè

The sound of my phone ringing took me away from my blank stare.

"Here they go with something else for me to do." I rolled my eyes as I saw that it was a call from the church. "First Lady Morray," I put on my professional voice. Yes, professional because this felt like a job.

"Yes, First Lady. This is Sister Melinda Christy. I was calling to remind you about the upcoming trustee board meeting. With your husband being away you need to play more of an active role. We are going through a lot to keep your husband in his position. This goes much deeper than us. I also needed to speak with you-"

I had to cut her off because she was speaking too fast. "What do you mean this goes much deeper than you all? Actually, I do play an active role. I am there every Sunday. Front row at that. My child and I."

"Yea. That is what else I wanted to speak with you about. You need to allow Denise to go to the church's nursery. That's government funded and you not placing your child in there is not a good look. I know you may be too young, but just….just be like

Geneva. Put the church before yourself. Be Christ like." I had to

take the phone away from my ear because I know she didn't just

say what I think I heard.

See this was my problem with this damn church or should

I say scam. Everything was about a damn image. Not about

praising God or being there for one another, but about a damn

image. Since my husband went away I've been trying to do what

I was supposed to do, but it was members like her that made me

want to leave the church, but I knew my hands were tied. On top

of that did this woman just said I should be more like Geneva?

"Let me tell you something. I don't know what Geneva

did, but I ain't her and I will never be her. All you will get out of

me is what I am giving so far. Now don't call my phone again

because obviously, you forgot what it meant to be a Christian. I

am hella crazy and it wouldn't mean anything to me to call up the

IRS and have the entire church audited. You forgot that you told

me you are on payroll. Don't try me sweetheart. I promise you that this young thing isn't what you want." I hung up the phone

and slammed it down on the island.

This was my final straw with this church thinking they

were going to just use me to be a part of their damn show. Half of

the members in that church were going to hell anyways. Kedra

instructed her girls to go back to the playroom and moved Denise

to her other hip.

"I'm telling you that something is up with that church.

It's like they want you to go above and beyond for them. Not

saying you aren't supposed to, but they teach you so wrong. They

made your pregnancy a living hell. Also, let us not forget that

somebody from that church sent that damn formula here and had

my little cousin close to death."

With every word she spoke, my head moved in

agreement. I was still trying to see who in the hell hurt my baby,

but the members of the trustee board swore to me that no one

from the church would do such a thing, but hell that church was

capable of everything.

Helena came into the kitchen with her hands on her hips.

"I can't find that damn piece of paper and I give up. What are y'all talking about in here and when are we going to get something to eat? I skipped breakfast."

"Senior told me where it is, but the church just called. Telling me I need to be more like Geneva."

"Like a dead woman? They want you to be more like the gay woman? That evil woman is who they want you to be more like? Please. I say you leave the church." Helena spoke while getting a can of soda from my fridge. "Y'all want something?"

Kedra and I shook our heads. My mind was still thinking about the conversation and my husband. Food was probably what I needed. It always made me feel better. "You know I can't leave the church, but we can go get something to eat after I feed Denise." My child must've knew it was feeding time because she reached her arms out to me.

"She's too greedy, but honestly. God please forgive me for what I am about to say, but I think Geneva got what she deserved by being killed. She was so spiteful," Kedra passed me

my child and took her phone out of her pocket.

Since it was just my girls and I, I felt free to just feed

without a covering. "Geneva was a real animal. I don't think she

should've been murdered, but the world is a better place without

her. I wish it would've happened a long time ago." We all fell out

laughing, but I kept my eye on Denise. It was beautiful to see

how she found my nibble.

"You don't have to say it, but I'm glad someone took her

out because God knows I wanted to. I don't think your husband

did it though. At least she's out of our hair and hopefully in hell."

Helena brought the can up to her lips.

Although none of us had said this aloud before. I was sure

we all wanted to say this a long time ago. Not that we were evil

people, but Geneva was no saint and it was good to know she

would never become a problem again.

"Oh that's how you feel for real Morray?" I heard the

voice before I looked up and saw the face, but I knew who it was.

I knew that voice better than I knew my own.

DJ was standing in my kitchen with a look of

disappointment on his face. I knew he felt some type of way

about his mother, but nobody wanted to hear that someone else

wanted their mother dead. "David, please. I didn't mean it like

that. Please." I started walking over to him, but he turned and

walked away.

"No. I knew my mother was a monster, but damn. I

thought you had some respect because of your love for me." He

was walking faster than I could keep up while I had a baby

latched on to me.

He swung open the front door and walked outside. "Let

me explain David. Geesh! Stop walking and let me talk to you."

"No. You was talking enough up in there with your little

friends. I came four hours to tell you that Markia said she loved

me, but I couldn't say it back to her because I am still in love

with you. Man, you aren't any better than my mother." He got

into his car and drove off.

That was a damn low blow and he knew it. He knew

telling me I was like his mother was going to hurt me, and he was right. It stung because I had worked so hard not to end up like

her. On top of that the fact that he was still in love with me left

me speechless because I loved him too, but there was nothing I

could do about that now. He was done with me and I was

married.

When I got back inside of the house Helena was standing

in the foyer and Kedra was fussing at her oldest daughter for

opening the door. By passing the both of them I headed towards

my room. I just wanted to be alone, and when my behind landed

on my bed, I realized that my child had never stopped feeding.

"Nessie you had to have been starving, huh Mommy?"

She was the reason why I was still here. If she was never

conceived the possibility that David and I could have worked it

out was probably higher than fifty percent. Denise was my

guardian angel and I just prayed she kept her mommy on the right

track. As she fed, she closed her eyes and relaxed herself, making

me to relax as well, but that was short lived.

"Are you ok? We heard what he said and we want you to

know that you were not wrong for what you said nor are you

anything like that damn witch." Helena came to comfort me with

Kedra.

Both of them sat down on the bed near me and kept trying

to make me feel better, but I was already good. It made me feel

good to know that David still had feelings for me. Even if he was

upset and I wasn't willing to act on my own feelings, I found

comfort that he still thought of me in that way.

For the rest of the day the girls, the kids, and I all lounged

around my house. We ordered Dristil's to go through Uber Eats

and just tried to keep our minds off of all of our problems.

Jameson came got the license, but said he wasn't sure if he even

needed it anymore which pissed me off even more. Senior never

called me back, and I didn't expect him to.

Chapter Five

David Jr.

After I left Morray's house, I drove around the city for hours. Just driving, smoking, and thinking. I know I had my own opinions about my mother, but that was the thing, she was my mother. I had the right to say anything about her that I chose, but no one else could. Not even the son of a dog that was married to her for over twenty years.

My mind was all over the place, but I figured I would pass by Kimora's dorm. Recently she had hit me up telling me she was in a bind and that she needed some money. At first I didn't want to give it to her, but I figured she'd exhausted all of her options if she was calling me. She told she was pregnant, but we both agreed that it was best if she aborted that thing. Giving all of the secrets that had been revealed to us, who knew what that child could have been born with. We hadn't spoken in a few months, but since I did have the cash she was asking for, I was just gonna drop by and give it to her.

"Hey DJ!" A group of girls all spoke as I got out of my car. I knew them all from church, but they were the group of fast girls. Every church had them and they all hung together.

"What's good y'all?" I waved and kept it going, but one of them broke away from the pack and headed my way.

Her name was Naomi and baby girl was fine as hell. I hit it from time to time, but that was about it. Again, she was a part of the fast girls. "DJ I wanted to talk to you about something."

"What is it Naomi?" We were standing in front of Kimora's building and I was hoping nobody saw us. Not that Markia would find out since she was in Miami, but I just didn't want anyone to get the wrong impression.

Naomi got closer to me and looked me over before licking her lips. "Well I was down at the nail salon the other day and I saw this white girl who was big pregnant, and she was telling her friend about her baby daddy. His name just so happens to be David Martin Jr., and they owned this big church out here in Tampa."

"What is your question Naomi?"

"You got a white girl pregnant?" She crossed her arms and pressed her lips together. "A white girl?"

I just laughed at her question because there was no reason for me to explain anything to her. Crazy thing about it though was that Hannah and I weren't even communicating. I just told her to call me whenever she went into labor.

"Naomi, what are you mad because it wasn't you?" I stood up straight and watched as she looked back at her girls. "I'm talking to you. Not your friends."

"Well I just wanted to know, but I guess I got my answer. Have fun being a baby daddy." She flipped her blonde weave towards me and walked away.

I laughed as I made my way inside of the dorm. I know that she came at me hoping to see if she could get some information out of me, but she wasn't. My business was my business, and I for sure was not about to broadcast that I got someone pregnant from a one nightstand. Hell, it wasn't even during the booty call hours. I got Hannah pregnant from a quickie.

When I got up to Kimora's floor, I felt uneasy. Like something was wrong, but I didn't know what. It could've been because of the thing with Morray, but I felt really nervous or like my mind was trying to tell me something, but it wasn't clear. I tried my hardest to think about what could be wrong, but I couldn't think of anything and someone had answered the door as soon as I knocked.

If I wasn't already angry with Morray, I know I was livid with Kimora for having this nigga answer her door. "I have every right to beat the hell out of you right now. You know that huh dawg?" I turned my lip up at my supposed to be best friend who was answering my ex's door in just his boxers.

Lloyd looked spook. He didn't know for sure if I was going to fight him or not, but I know that he knew that our friendship was over. "Look DJ I can explain all of this. It didn't even start off like this. We were just chillin, and if you talking about that drug stuff. Man I had no idea it was going to cause an accident. I swear you know you are my nigga."

Kayla Andrè

As my brain was trying to process the information he was telling me, my fist reacted faster than I did and collided with his mouth. I just kept ig going. Kept hitting him in his head, even after he had fallen to the floor. I felt a wetness on my hand, but I never stopped going because the more my mind processed the words he had spoken, the harder I went.

My own best friend had given me the drug that had caused me to almost lose my life. Even when I was in the hospital I denied all of their proof of a drug being in my system because I knew that I had never taken one, but to find out my best friend and my girl at the time set me up killed me.

"What is going on? DJ stop he's not moving! Stop it!" I felt Kimora come up behind me, but I had a problem with her too. I swung my hand back to get her off of me, but I didn't know my own strength because I heard her crash into the wall.

I did stop hitting Lloyd because I saw how badly he looked on the floor. His face was covered in blood and I knew already his lip was bust and his nose had to be broken. Looking at

Kimora's desk that was near us and grabbed her drying towel off

the back of the chair to wipe my hands off. I hated them.

My disdain for Lloyd was much stronger than that for

Kimora because he was supposed to be my brother, and not only

did he drug me, but he was sleeping with Kimora, and it seemed

to have started months ago.

"What is wrong with you? You just came in here and beat

him up? Are you jealous of us? You still want me or something.

That little dark girl ain't enough for you?" Kimora rushed to help

Lloyd, but something about her was different. Her face was much

fatter than normal.

"You kept that baby Kimora? You are still pregnant after

you found out the sick truth?" My hand found its way around her

neck. Lloyd was groaning in pain, but he'd have to suffer because

I had another problem on my hands.

Kimora eye's damn near popped out of her head, but she

was started to swing her hands to hit me. "This ain't your damn

Baby! It's his!" She coughed up some mucus and spit it into my

face.

In that moment I realized why I never wanted to deal with Kimora to begin with. She was something like my mother. She demonic as one could possible get. "Man look this here is crazy. I can't stand neither one of y'all and I pray that karma gets you both, but I promise you that every time I see that nigga, I'll beat the hell out of him. As for you Kimora, I got someone for you too."

Slamming my foot into Lloyd's rib once more, I decided that enough was enough, for today and I needed to get out of there before they called the police or worse. "Who your new little girlfriend? She'll never be me. You can never replace me."

"You are sick you know that. We now know we are siblings and you are still thinking I want you in that way? But no, I got someone else for you. Someone we both know you could never measure up against." There was a knock on the door. From the sound of it, it sounded like someone who was trying to see what all was going on.

Usually I knew my father would always be able to bail me out, but with him being in jail and not being able to bail him own self out, I knew I needed to get ghost. I opened the door and saw

Naomi standing there. Should have known that she and Kimora

were roommates. Birds of a feather flocked together.

"Who you got for me?" Kimora choked up once I had

stepped into the hallway. I looked back into the room and saw the

morbid sight that I had caused. Lloyd was still laying on the floor

with Kimora sitting right beside him, still rubbing her neck.

Naomi looked from each one of us to the other, trying to piece

together what could have happened in her head.

Cracking a smile, I answered her question. "Morray."

Chapter Six

Pastor David

"I'm surprised you called this meeting with me David. Are you ready to confess?" Miranda waltzed into our usual meeting room with her behind sticking in the air. I didn't speak any words, but I watched as she sat down with a smile on her face and a folder and a pen in hand. She kept her eyes locked me as well. "Well speak because that's the only freedom you'll have for the rest of your life."

It amazed me how she could keep this act up about me murdering Geneva, knowing all along that I didn't do it. This was her way of punishing me for not wanting to be with her, and I also believed it was one of God's sick jokes or just His way of coming back at me for all of the things that I've done wrong.

I missed my wife and I missed my child. I was ready to get out of this place so I know what I needed to do. So as she went on her rant, I gathered my words. "I'm ready to be with you."

Her entire demeanor changed. She went from being the know-it-all to being an actual woman and knowing her place.

"Well, I'm happy about that. I guess you've learned your lesson."

Miranda got up from the table and walked over to me. I've never had a problem getting up. Matter of fact, I prided myself about the stamina I had, but Miranda was no Morray so I wasn't the least bit aroused. Yea, I slept with Miranda before hand, but being in here made me realize how much I never wanted to mess up what I had at home.

"What's going on here? Come on let's get out of these clothes so I can see how your fine body."

As I begin to undress I reminded myself why I was doing this and imagined it was Morray I was sneaking around with. Miranda got down in front of me, taking my member in her hand and placing it into her mouth. I won't lie to you and say that the warmth and wetness she was providing me was well needed since I hadn't been inside of something in about six, almost seven, months.

Kayla Andrè

When I looked down, our eyes met, so I hurried to close mine. Picturing that it was Morray on her knees before me, pleasing me. While Miranda bobbed her head back and forth, she slowly slid her hands from my shaft to my thighs, before she starting moaning really loudly. "Don't do that!" I pulled at her hair, forcing her to stop.

I kept her down there until I was on the edge of releasing in the back of her throat before I stood her up and bent her over the table. Ramming myself inside of her, raw, but I knew how to hold on. There was no way I would chance getting her pregnant, but at her age I doubt if she was still able to get pregnant.

Miranda was more of a freak than I remembered because she asked for me to shove myself in her backdoor. It surprised me because the last person I had done that with was Geneva and it didn't go too well, but that didn't matter this time because as soon as I went in Miranda started to moan my name. Her body was so curvy that while I was working her insides, I became fascinated at how round she was. My wife was plump, but she was not this curvy.

Because I was hitting her from behind, I could've just stayed in, but I didn't want to do that. I wanted to remind her that even with me being on the inside, she was still just a pawn to me. With that thought in mind, I pulled out and turned her around, jerking myself off so that I could get all of it. When I started to skeet out, I made sure to cover every inch of her face.

"Why would you do that when you know I don't have anything to wipe it off with, and if I did, I'm at work for Christ's sake. I'll be wiping all of my makeup off." Miranda sat on her knees with her shoulders up in the air.

Handing her my boxers, I sat down on the chair and waited patiently while she cleaned her face as best as she could. "So about my release?" Even though I did climax, I still had a goal behind it. I needed to get out of here. Get to my family, my wife.

"When I leave here, I'll head to my office and draft up the paperwork, but this isn't over. Even when you get out we will continue this." She threw the boxers back at me and kissed my lips. I didn't know how much makeup she was wearing originally, but even after she wiped her face, it looked fully done to me.

I already knew that she would make me continue this once I was out, but I already had a plan on how to get out of that too. All I needed to do was get out of here so that I could get back to running things. Not that I had lost my touch on the outside, but it wasn't like I wanted it to be since I wasn't there to make sure things were being done the way I wanted them to be done.

"I know, but I need to get out of here. Don't play with me. You got what you wanted, now give me what I want." I turned in my seat and watched as she pulled her skirt down and made her way to the door to exit.

"David, I know. I will get you out of here. I'm actually ready to get this case off of my desk anyway. Just stay in here Babe. I'll have an officer bring you more clothes." She blew me a kiss and was out.

Finally, God was starting to actually do something that was going to benefit me instead of having me benefit everyone else.

****

Today was the day. The day that I was going to go before the judge and Miranda was going to say that an error occurred during the investigation and I was no longer a suspect. It took her two days to get this together, and I was more than excited. I didn't even tell Morray I was getting out yet. The only two people who did know was Troy and Jameson.

I was transferred to a holding cell in the court early in the morning. Miranda had come back to visit me last night to get off once more and to also make sure that I remembered that once I was out that we still needed to continue to do what we were doing. I made love to her just so she knew I was willing to do whatever in order to get out of here.

Although I did tell her we could continue, in the back of my mind I had other plans for her. I was going to use the connections I had in order to make sure she was out of a job. It was one thing to falsely accuse someone of a crime, but it

something totally different to accuse the person in order to get

them to have sex with you.

Honestly, I didn't even know why Miranda had become

that desperate. She was a beautiful woman and even with her age

she had kept herself up. I was more than sure that if she were to

stop being such a slut she would be able to marry or get with

anyone she wanted; besides me of course.

"Inmate the judge will see you now." A prison guard

came to open my cell. Surprisingly, he didn't know who I was so

he wasn't as easy going with me as he should have been. Hell,

usually the guards on the inside would pick me up from

breakfast, but this man just shoved a plate with a cold sandwich

on it into my cell this morning.

Nonetheless, I excused his rudeness and made my way

towards him so that he could cuff me and lead me out. There was

a smile plastered on my face because I knew I was only about

five minutes away from being totally free.

I didn't care if they had another suspect in mind to solve Geneva's murder or not, but as long as it was not me. Hell, even with being in jail for her murder, she wasn't on my mind. I didn't like her when I was married to her and I despised her even more now.

When my eyes saw the doors of the courtroom, I felt weak. Everything started to move in slow motion. The noise around sounded as if it was being slowed down as well. My legs felt as if they didn't want to move anymore. On the inside, I began to panic because I didn't know what was going on.

"Walk straight inmate." The guard yelled at me and shoved me, but even that seemed to go in slow motion. He acted as if I wanted to stumble when I walked, but I couldn't help it. I took one more step and I felt my body go numb, causing me to fall to the ground. "Help! Somebody call an ambulance. We have an inmate down."

Chapter Seven

First Lady Morray

When I tell you the last thing I wanted to be doing with my time was spending it a damn trustee meeting, but here I was pulling into my designated parking spot. Kedra had asked to keep Denise overnight last night and as badly as I wanted to say no, I decided that it would be a good chance for me to catch up on some much-needed rest. I thought my husband would call this morning and we'd have a hot session of phone sex, but that was wishful thinking because there were no collect calls.

Coming to this church I had to go above and beyond to slay because if I didn't I knew it would be discussed. So, I decided on a pair of distressed jeans, a sheer cream top that fell off my shoulder, and a pair of nude high-arch stilettos. My natural hair had been blown out by the Brazilians so that was taken care of, and my makeup was poppin. I knew I was cute and the people who turned their heads when I walked by knew it as well.

Sister Christy stopped me as soon as I walked into the conference room. "First Lady can I speak to you please?" She pulled me by my arm slightly and led me to the side. This woman was becoming a thorn in my side.

"How may I help you?" I looked down at her hand that was still on my arm. Catching on, she quickly removed her hand.

"Do you think it's appropriate to wear this in the house of God?" She turned her nose up as she studied my outfit even more. There was nothing I could do, but laugh. The rips in my pants weren't inappriate because you could barely see my skin and I wore a tank underneath my sheer shirt. Yea my shoulders were out, but this was the same woman who was damn near fifty wearing a crop top to the church's picnic.

Pushing my hair out of my face, I smiled and walked away from her. She clearly was threatened by me and I was more than sure she'd been with my husband. She was just too pressed about me, and I had been around long enough to know when women got like that it normally had to do with *your* man.

Kayla Andrè

Taking my place at the head of the table, where I had been forced to sit every time I came to one of these things, I crossed my legs and called for the meeting to begin. I actually like the fact that I was in charge. I didn't know what the hell I was doing, but I knew that I was in charge of something.

As they begin to discuss the who was getting paid what and how many of the church's rental properties needed renovations, I scanned the room for Troy, but he wasn't there which was odd. Normally he would be here in the chair next to me since he was acting pastor, but he wasn't here for this meeting.

"First Lady Martin how do you feel about this?" I looked up and all eyes were on me. I didn't know who'd called out for my attention, hell I didn't know what they were even talking about at that point.

"Can you repeat the last part please?" I scratched my head and plastered a smile on my face.

I noticed Sister Christy roll her eyes, but it was another lady that actually spoke up. "We wanted to know if your family would be ok if your husband's salary was cut in half since he

isn't fulfilling his duties."

I cocked my head to the side to see if they were serious.

When nobody laughed, I realized that they really thought this was

going to fly, but oh how wrong they were. At a normal church, I

would be ok with this because I knew they were doing things

decently and in order, but see this little scam operation they had

going on didn't do anything decently.

"No we wouldn't be ok." I sat up in the chair so they

could see I wasn't playing. "If my husband's salary has to be cut

that means the man who runs the money to the bank's salary

needs to be cut. The Sunday school teachers don't really need to

be on payroll anyways since normally that is a job you volunteer

to do. Sister Christy, you wouldn't mind your salary being cut in

half either am I correct? I mean seriously, do we really need to

get paid to say the church's announcements?"

The room fell silent as everyone looked around the room

so they wouldn't have to make eye contact with me. I was ready

to go in some more because to me it was really disrespectful that the church's money was going to things that it didn't need to go

to. I mean yes, the church was massive so there were many

programs to help the public, but they were too busy paying

salaries to everyone who picked up a piece of paper.

Sister Christy picked up the meeting, changing the subject

to something totally different so I sat back and relaxed myself.

My escape came sooner than I expected when Ms. Dorothy asked

to speak with me outside. Before I left I grabbed my purse and

phone because I knew I was not coming back.

"Hey what's wrong?" I closed the door behind us and

took a look at her face. She was looking down at the floor,

twiddling her fingers. "Ms. Dorothy?"

She jumped a little when I placed my hand on her

shoulder. "There was an emergency. Pastor, pastor. Your

husband was rushed to Memorial." I felt my body become

uneasy. I heard what she said, but I wasn't understanding her.

"What do you mean?" I searched my purse for my phone.

"W-why would he be there?" I couldn't find the phone and I

knew I had just threw it in the bag so it should be on top, but I couldn't find it.

My anxiety was getting the best of me and somehow the purse managed to fall out of my hands and onto the floor spilling some of the things I held inside. I bent down to pick them up, but the tears were starting to form at the bottom of my eyes, making it hard for me to see.

"First Lady let me help you." Dorothy got down on her knees beside me trying to help me out. When my phone started to ring, I grabbed it from the floor and answered.

"Hello?" My voice was shaky and my vision was too blurry to look at the screen.

"Morray. I need you to get down to Memorial now. David collapsed on his way to court. Just get here and I'll explain."

Ms. Dorothy handed me my purse and keys separately. I was on my way out the door when I realized Troy said my husband was on the way to court. "What in the hell do you mean he was on his way to court? Why was I not notified that he had court today? Don't you think I would have wanted to be there?"

This was the first real court date he would have had and if it meant he was closer to coming home, then of course I wanted to be there. I was practically running towards my car.

"I promise I will explain everything once you are here, but please get here. They won't let me act on his behalf because I'm not family. Just come on Morray."

"Yea, I'm on my way now. It shouldn't take me any longer than fifteen minutes to get there."

Once I reached my truck, I pushed the button to turn it on, and backed out of my parking spot and headed towards the hospital. As rocky as things have been between Senior and I, I knew that if something happened to him it would mess me up. What would that mean for my daughter, or myself?

I kept my phone on my lap as I sped down the interstate to the other side of town. My heart was pounding fast and I felt as if I still wasn't getting there fast enough. While I tried to keep calm, but it wasn't working so I said a quick prayer for the man in my life.

As I pulled into the parking lot of the hospital, God had saved me a parking spot right by the door. I pressed the button to turn my car off, but the vibration of my leg stopped me from getting out right away. I hadn't seen the number on the screen in a long time, but I had an idea what the text was going to read.

"Sorry for your husband's illness, but you better hope it's not an STD since he an habitual cheater."

That pissed me off. Hell almost made me not want to go inside the hospital because with Senior being distant it wasn't hard to believe he wasn't cheating on me. Being in jail wouldn't stop him. There were female guards and I already had a feeling that he was messing with that DA.

Nonetheless, I decided to make my way up. I had to call Troy again and ask him where to go. Once getting off the elevator on the fifth floor, it didn't take long for me to find the room. There were two officers standing on each side of the door with Troy standing on the other side.

"Where is he? What's going on? Where is the doctor?" I tried to look into the room, but the curtain was pulled. I went to walk to through the door, but the officers moved closer together and blocked my entrance. "He's my husband! Move out of my way." I pushed them, and these grown men really pushed me back.

"Aye man don't be touching her. You must not know who that is in that room." Troy came and stopped me from falling. The officers looked at each other and got back in their positions, but I knew they weren't going to let me in until they realized who I was.

"Troy where is Jameson? He needs to be here because these stupid heathens over here don't know my husband. What are they doing to him?" I turned my back to the men and folded my arms. I wasn't panicking as much as I was since I had received that text.

Of course Troy had his phone in his hand and he was texting away. "He is coming. They are supposed to be dropping the charges against him today. Just stay here and wait until the doctor's come and let them know who you are."

I just nodded my head and took up some wall space next to him. I was excited to hear Senior was going to be free. Maybe we could get back to where we were. I had to laugh myself after that thought. After I got to the bottom of these texts, I was sure we would never be where we once were again.

Chapter Eight

David Jr.

I had gone ghost for a couple of days, not trying to be around anyone. I decided to talk to my professors and somehow convince me to finish their classes online. I mean my mother died for Christ's sake. While I was in Miami, Kia showed up in my dorm room trying to get me to talk to her, but I wasn't trying to talk to her. We did end up sleeping together though, but I had to leave Miami and be back home in Tampa and since I had been here, Hannah's house had been where I was staying.

"So I was thinking we could take some maternity pictures. I saw a couple of Facebook that I liked. When do you think you would want to take them?" Hannah sat at the breakfast table in front of me with her phone in her hand.

Being here with her was weird because we were never in a relationship. Hell we never even got to the level where we were *"talking"*. So being here with her, in her house, sleeping in her bed, and her trying have sex with me every chance she had was strange, but not uncomfortable. I knew for a fact that I would never be with her, but I was cool with her for now.

She handed me her phone so that I could see the pictures she was talking about. They looked cute, but each one of these ladies looked as if they were happily committed with the man they were taking the picture with. I knew what Hannah was doing, and I wasn't for it.

"I'll pay for you to take the pictures, but I don't want to be in them like these men are." I handed her the phone and went back to my cereal.

"Is this how you are going to act this entire time? Are you going to act like this for the rest of her lives? I know that you didn't want to be with me, but here we are, together. We are here expecting a child together. We might as well get married."

Her words caused a natural reaction of me choking on the fruit loops that were in my mouth. "Hannah how did that thought ever come across your mind. I'm here because I needed a place to crash, but if you think that I'm here to try something out with you, I'm not."

I hated to be so harsh, but I wasn't going to lie to her and have her in her feelings. Although I felt like she was going to be in them either way. I watched as she sunk in her seat and closed her phone before placing it on the table. Honestly, I started to feel bad for being so harsh. She looked sad in her face.

"You want me to leave and go somewhere else?" I cleaned up my mess and got up from the table, but I watched her as I went to the sink. She shook her head no and picked up her phone again. "Well what do you want Hannah? I won't marry you if I feel like my heart isn't in it, and as of right now my heart ain't in it. Hell, I don't know if my heart will ever be in it."

She stood up from her seat and walked towards me, placing her phone down on the counter. "Look I never had the two-parent household, and I know you think I trapped you, but I promise you I didn't. I just want her to live a life I never lived. A life like you did, you know?" She folded her arms and looked down at the ground.

"How do you even know anything about me anyways? I never told you who I was or where I came from? All you knew was I played football and got into an accident. Which I now

know my fake friends and ex-girlfriend caused." I threw in the

last part just for myself because I needed to keep telling myself

that because it still didn't seem real.

"DJ you act like it's hard for someone in Tampa not to

know whose child you are. The entire city knows who your father

is rather they want to admit it or not. Just because I'm white

doesn't mean anything. My mom used to attend your father's

service sometimes, but after my uncle started a church she left

your father's church and started going there."

I was shocked to hear her words because all my life I

knew my father was popular, but I didn't think I would meet

someone of the opposite race who knew who he was like talking

about it. I began to wash off my bowl and spoon, not knowing

how to really reply to her. I felt for her because I didn't want this

little girl growing up the way I did and she didn't want the child

growing up the way she did.

"My life wasn't all it was cracked up to be. Yea I had two

parents, but they weren't there for me. They were all about the church. I practically raised myself. Then after all of this time I find out that my father isn't my father. My father is my ex-girlfriend's father. My life is screwed up so trust me when I say you don't want to raise this baby the way I was raised."

Thinking of my life made me upset because all of the lies I had been told all of my life. There was no way I would allow that to happen to my unborn.

"Yea, but you had money. I put myself through school and worked my tail off to get everything I have. I don't want my child to go through that." Her voice rose a little bit, she still tried not to yell.

With that answer, I knew what this was all was about for her. She wanted the money. I can't say for sure she trapped me, but I knew that she didn't sleep with me by chance. She wanted a better life for herself and I can't say that I blamed her. Money made the world go around. I knew that and I had money, so I could only imagine how a person would feel if they didn't have it.

"Well if that's your major concern, you don't have to stress. The baby will be a Martin. She'll be well taken care of." I placed my hand on her shoulder to assure her before I walked off. My phone was ringing on the table.

When I picked it up, the number wasn't saved so I chanced it and answered it. "Who is this?"

"DJ, don't hang up, but it's Steven, you're father."

"Man you ain't ever been a father to me." I stopped him before he could go any further.

"Just listen.. I want to at least meet up with you. I want to make this right."

I considered saying *no* because honestly my mindset was *"eff him,"* but something told me to at least give him a shot. Neither of my family parents were what they were supposed to be, so maybe he would turn out different. I agreed to meet up with him in an hour at a local bar in town. It was still early, but this bar was twenty-four hours and they had the best hot wings.

I was late on purpose. Not too late, but late enough for anyone to think their time wasn't being valued because his wasn't. When I walked in, he was already sitting at the bar with a mug of beer and a big plate of wings. I just sat down next to him on the stool, not really greeting him until I got comfortable.

"I'm glad you took the time out to meet me because I do know how you feel and I just want to talk to you so that you could understand my side of things." Steven pushed his plate of food my way, but I just shook my head, declining his offer.

"Yea, well with everything going on, I figured I could give you a chance. I don't want you to think I'm here looking for you to just be my father. I'm just here to get some understanding."

Steven didn't say anything, but he did acknowledge me with a head nod. It fell silent for a few minutes because I guess neither one of us knew where to start. I almost felt like a little boy because I didn't know how to open my mouth to say what I felt. I wasn't necessarily hurt, but more so disappointed. Thinking about how my entire life is a lie and they all of them had a hand in making my life this way.

I've always been taught that God did everything for a reason, but how many damn reasons does there need to be. Nothing was going right, and besides football and school, my life was shambled. Technically I didn't have a mother anymore, I was having a baby by a girl I damn for sure wasn't feeling, and on top of all of that the only girl I loved was married to my father. I don't care what anyone says, God be playing with me.

After I ordered my food I was more comfortable with talking and saying what was on my mind. "So didn't even think I could be yours? I mean maybe once or twice I was told I resembled my dad, but that was about it. Now that I look at you, we actually do favor a lot." Before I arrived I looked at his Facebook page and saw myself in him. I don't know if it was my emotions or if it was actually true, but I know what I saw.

"Honestly, after Geneva told me that you weren't mine, I just let it go. Did I have a thought? Yea, a few times, but I was so stuck on myself back then that I didn't want my infidelities to come out. Then when I looked at you, you had him. David was one of the most powerful men in this city. He could give you things that I couldn't. I thought I was doing what was best, but now I wish I would have acted because looking at things, I was wrong and I am so sorry for that."

Hearing him apologize almost felt like a weight was being lifted off of my shoulders. Nobody has ever just told me they were sorry and he did. He was really the last person who actually needed to apologize to me, but I appreciated it.

"Thank you," was all that needed to be said. He didn't need me to curse him out and fight him because he understood. This situation was as sick as one could be and he got it and he apologized for it. That allowed me to have some respect for him.

Kimora wasn't a subject that I wanted to bring up, so after Steven said he was sorry we just ate our food and discussed the things that were going on in the world of sports. Altogether it was a good time. I laughed for a long time in a long time. Not to mention he knew the bartender so I was getting beer underage. I was already doing it while I was at school, but hell it felt good to be doing it out in the open.

Right before I was about to get into my car, Steven said

he had something else he wanted to tell me. "What's good?" I

looked around the parking lot kind of confused because I didn't

know what he had to say that he couldn't have said the two hours

we were in the bar.

He looked around and started acting really nervous. "I

spoke with your mom right before her death." Steven just stopped

in the middle of his sentence.

"Ok and? What did she say?" I walked closer to him.

Since he was a few feet away from me, standing behind my car.

"She wanted me to tell you that Kimora needed to keep

the baby. I cursed her out for even thinking like that, but in the

end she said something about how all the truth will come out

sooner than later, but in order for you to achieve your destiny,

Kimora needed the baby. I was told Kimora had an abortion so

it's too late to do anything. I'm glad she didn't keep that devil

baby. This stuff really is disgusting and all of it could have been

avoided if I did my part."

Kayla Andrè

My mother always found ways to outdo herself. Even though she knew that Kimora and I were siblings, she still wanted me to have a baby with this girl? Geneva Martin was the true definition of evil and I'm starting to think I got mad Morray a little too quickly because in a way she was right.

"I know it's hard to process, but I just felt like I needed to let you know. I know you don't need another parent, but I would like to build some sort of relationship with you. I got two little girls now and I would like them to have a big brother, even if you don't call me Dad."

"This ain't just on you. It's mainly on my mother because she was the one pulling the strings." I paused to spit because that's how I felt about my mom at that moment. "As for Kimora, you will become a grandfather either way. She never got the abortion, but she says I'm not the father. Some dude I used to call my brother is."

Steven's eyes grew buck when I said that. I knew I had just threw something unexpected at him. I just wanted to get out

there and get somewhere because my mind was going in all sorts
of directions.

Unlocking my car doors, I went to get inside. "Aye, and
yea I would like to meet your kids. I never had siblings so it'd be
nice to have some now since I ain't got nothing else." Steven just
nodded his head and my direction and I got in my car.

Sometimes I thought it would be easier to just end all of
this. No, it would be best if I ended it all. Seemed like God was
allowing the devil to have a field day with my life. Like He was
allowing the devil to test me like he did Job. Take everything
away from me, and although I hate to admit it, this dude was
winning because I give up. I was in the right mind to go to the
church and get the gun out of my father's old office. Nobody
knew it was there, but me. Maybe a few other deacons, but I
knew it wasn't many people because the congregation would
have a fit to know that the pastor was keeping a glock underneath
his desk at the church.

Speeding like a bat out of hell, I was hitting the interstate
hard because I wanted all of this to be over. This life of mine

wasn't worth it. The funny part was that the closer I got to the church, the more it felt like God was talking to me, but hell it was too late. God wasn't messing with me when my momma was running around ruining my life. He damn for sure wasn't there when my best friend started messing around with my girlfriend.

As soon as I pulled up to the church, I noticed that only a few cars where there. Most likely it was just the cleaning committee. I parked in my usual spot and went in through the side door. Although it was locked, I knew the access code.

My adrenaline had me going because I was slipping through these hallways like a Cheshire cat. One of the men who was cleaning the church turned the corner and we bumped into each other. "My bad Brother Martin. I didn't even know you were here." He bent down to start picking up the things he dropped. I bent down to pick up a can and handed it to him. Not really trying to make conversation. "You need help with something?"

"Nah, I got it." I pushed past him so I could get to the office. Like I thought nobody was there. I slipped in and went right behind the desk. It was supposed to be right underneath the top of the desk, on the right side, almost halfway to the back, and in a plastic holster.

On my knees, I started feeling around and I couldn't find it. Panic started to set in so I took my phone out to use the light from it. *Where in the hell is this thing?* My heart felt like it was pumping harder and faster. My mind was moving all over trying to find this thing, but thanks to the light I spotted it. Some idiot had moved it to the left side. Most likely it was Troy.

Getting it down, I placed it in my lower back and straighten up the little that I did mess up. I got out of that church like a bat out of hell. My mind was calculating the best place for me to do it. It had to be done at my old house because that's where all of these skeletons are. That place housed all of the demons.

The house wasn't too far from the church, but it was far enough where I needed to get back on the interstate. The music was off so when the vibration of my phone sounded out in the cup holder, I heard it. Looking down I saw it was Morray. She was the reason behind this too. After what she'd done to me, she deserved to cry at my funeral. I loved that girl with everything in me, and she slept with my father. I don't care whatever her reasoning was. She slept with him and created a child.

Pulling up to the house, I parked the car. Since my mother had been gone they'd pad locked the doors and all. Supposedly they were going to clean it up and sell it, but I don't know what was up with that. Took me a second to realize that I was about to do this, but I was ready to leave this world of pain. They always said if I took my own life I would never make it to Heaven, but I was sure Hell wasn't as bad as the pain that I had endured.

Turning the car off, I decided that I was going to the back and do it there. Getting the gun out, I sat it on my lap and looked at it. This thing was my god for the moment. It held all the power that could take away my life in an instant. It was practically going to save me.

Just as I opened the door, my car started ringing and my phone started vibrating. My car wasn't on so this wasn't possible, but it was driving me insane. Causing me to get a migraine. It was almost like the movies where I knew the vein in my forehead was showing because it was hurting that badly.

"Stop! Stop it! Turn it off." I was pressing all kinds of random buttons trying to turn it off, but somehow the ringing turned into Morray's voice.

"David, I love you please just talk to me. Let me explain everything. Like I can't live this life without you and I know I was wrong, but please I don't want to live without you. Just come talk to me or I'll come to you. Please David, just don't be mad at me. I didn't mean it like that."

It became harder to breathe in that moment because it felt like I couldn't move. My back was stuck up against my seat, feeling as if someone had their hands in my chest, pushing me back. It seemed as if everything was going slower and slower. I saw a butterfly pass in front of my windshield, but it was moving so slow I got to see it flap its wings.

"David I know you are there. You don't have to say much, just say that you'll let me explain." I heard her whimpering. Even with that I couldn't say anything.

Kayla Andrè

My right hand picked up the gun, and as crazy as it sounds I know I didn't do it. I didn't even tell my hand to move, but it did. My hand picked up the gun and placed it up to my temple. The cold steel against my skin gave me the chills, but it didn't stop there. Before I could regain control of my own self, I pulled the trigger.

Click was all I heard. I didn't black out and I didn't feel blood, but my arm collapsed and fell on top of armrest. The gun fell out of my hand and into the other seat. I took the deepest breath I had ever taken in my life. When that oxygen hit my lungs, I felt alive or reborn.

"David. David what was that noise? David!" Morray spoke louder into the phone. I still wasn't sure how she was on the phone with me, but it didn't matter anymore. All the memories of what had just happened and what I had planned to do came back to me and the tears started to fall. I don't care what you say, I'll always believe that the same God I had cursed all those moments ago was the same God that was behind that bullet not being in my skull right now.

"I love you too." I managed to get that out, but I was still crying to hard. "God. Nobody, but God." I looked up and thanked Him.

Morray didn't say anything else. I'm sure she was confused with me crying and then just calling on God. She didn't hang up though. I went to start my car and realized that it was already on. Maybe I never turned it off or maybe this was God's way of telling me I needed to get out of there. Either way, I knew that I'd never disrespect Him like this again.

Chapter Nine

Pastor David

It never fails that while I'm trying to do right, something always comes along and messes me up. I've been in this damn hospital for a week with them trying to run tests and all to see why I fainted. My wife has dropped by once a day with Denise, but I feel like she was only coming so that I could see my child. Each time she came she sat by the couch underneath the window and played on her phone. When others would come to visit, she still stayed on her phone.

Today was no different. She'd come in, handed me some food and Denise before she went to sit down. I wasn't going to let her mess up my day though. Jameson went to court today on my behalf and they are supposed to be dropping the charges. Although they were supposed to be dropped a week ago, since I was in here and sick they pushed back the court date. Miranda had made it so that I didn't have to be shackled to the bed, but there was an officer to come by once a day to make sure I didn't go anywhere.

"Babe you think when I get out of here you and I can go somewhere, just us? Let us get back to the place we used to be?" I finally spoke up. Denise was sleeping on side of me and the room was eerie quiet.

Morray looked up from her phone and eyed me for a second before nodding her head. "Yea, we can do that." She looked away as soon as she said it, but still it made me smile. Even the thought of her loving me again made me feel just a little bit better.

Although that I was going to have to finish handling things with Miranda, that didn't need to take a toll on my marriage. I had big plans for when I got out. From handling things with the church to handling things with my family.

That was another thing on my mind. My mother had called bashing me because of my many screw-ups, but there was nothing she could do. I was now officially head of the family. So with that I needed to get my health back on track because I had plans for my family. Plans to make us wealthier, in the name of The Lord.

Troy walked into the room just as I was about to tell Morray something else. "Hey Troy!" My head turned in Morray's direction because she greeted him happier than she greeted me. I knew nothing was going on with them, but damn it did make me question myself.

"What's good Morray! How are you doing Pastor? I came through to check on you." He dapped me off and reached over me to grab Denise. "This has to be the world's healthiest baby. Morray what are you feeding this girl?"

Morray slipped her phone away and smiled up at him. "Troy don't play my baby. She's only being breastfed."

Troy walked over to sit next to her on the sofa. Now they weren't sitting too close, but hell he was still on that sofa and my wife was still smiling. So I pressed the button to rise my bed up so I could see and be a part of the conversation. "You know my wife is healthy herself." I smiled over at her, but she just looked at me.

It took me a while to catch on to the fact that I had just called my wife fat. Troy had started playing with Denise since he'd woke her up. "Baby you know you're the finest thing in all of America." I tried to make up for what I said earlier.

"Thanks," was all she said before she pulled back out her phone. Knowing that the conversation was done, I picked up my phone as well and started to read emails that I hadn't gone over.

Troy stayed for about an hour, He played with Denise and spoke to me about church business, but he and Morray didn't speak much. Until it was time for him to leave and she stood up to hug him and take Denise from him. He dapped me off and left. Morray had sat back down, placing a blanket over her shoulder and started to breastfeed our daughter.

"Are you cheating on me?" I placed my phone back down on the tray and waited for her to answer.

Before she answered me she flipped her hair and moved the blanket to check on Denise. "Senior you are the last person to be trying to ask me such a question."

"But are you? I just need to know because it seems as if you and I aren't even on the same page anymore."

"We aren't on the same page because you have been in jail. So like I said you are the last person that needs to be asking me a thing like that."

Now she was making me upset because I was her husband. I had every right in the world to be asking her if she was stepping out on me. Hell, I wouldn't be too wrong because she did sleep with me while she was supposed to be with my son, but oh how some people soon forget.

"Morray I love you ok. I just don't want us to have any problems. I want our family forever. I want to have more children with you so our legacy can live on." That was the truth. I loved her with everything I had left. Yes, I messed up a lot, but that doesn't mean I didn't love her. The devil was trying me and I'm working on making sure he didn't win the war.

She didn't respond to me, but she fixed herself so that she could be more comfortable while she had Denise in her arms. Watching their bond made the question of her cheating slide to the back of my head. Denise was everything to Morray and I knew she wouldn't want to mess up her daughter's perfect life so she wouldn't play me like that.

The knock on the door startled me. My doctor came into the room holding my chart in his hand. This man was new because Dr. Tanner was working out of state on some sort of research project. He told me that Dr. Andrews was the second-best doctor next to him. He was an older white man, but he seemed pretty cool.

"Mr. Martin how are you doing today? I see your wife is here. Hey Mrs. Martin." He nodded his head in her direction. I noticed that he wasn't as cheery as he usually was.

"We're good. How about you? You don't seem too happy."

Dr. Andrews looked back over at my wife and bit his bottom lip. "Mrs. Martin, do you mind stepping out for a moment please?"

My heart started to pump fast. What did he want to say that he felt as though he couldn't say it in front of my wife. "No, no doc. Whatever you have to say can be said in front of my wife."

"Ok, well we've been doing some tests and the results are starting to come in. We've found a tumor in your lungs, but we aren't sure if it is benign or malignant. We'd have to go in to get a sample. As of now you don't have to stay in the hospital anymore. I can discharge you and schedule some follow up appointments."

My head was spinning because this couldn't be true. There was no way that this was happening. A tumor? Like I said earlier, something always comes up. Morray had made her way over to me, with Denise on her shoulder, burping her.

"So what does this mean? Am I dying or something?" I grabbed my wife's hand for the needed support.

Dr. Andrews looked from me to my wife before he spoke again. "Honestly, I won't be able to know until we've gone in and gotten a sample. As of now I don't want you to worry. Leave here and enjoy your life."

I was at a loss for words. I just nodded my head and looked over at my wife. She was teary eyed herself. After a few seconds, Dr. Andrews left and told me he was going to get started on my discharge papers.

"How am I supposed to be enjoying life if there was a chance that I could be dying?" I scooted over in my bed to make room for my wife to sit down.

"Baby we will pray and trust God. He will lead you. He knows what's best. Just don't stress. It won't do you any good. How about we plan to take that trip? Once we beat these charges that is."

I still hadn't told her about me already getting off because I didn't want her to question it. I was just going to let Jameson tell her for me. Thankfully I didn't have to wait long because Jameson rushed through the door.

"Good afternoon! I'm just coming from court." His face was lit up. Probably because he knew he was getting paid. "This is for you." He handed me a piece of paper.

Morray looked over the paper with me. "What does this mean?" She looked over at him.

"This means your husband is a free man. The DA didn't have any evidence that connected him to the crime. Hell they don't even have a body."

Even with this news of me no longer being a suspect in my ex's murder, I still wasn't happy. All of five minutes ago I was told that I could have cancer. This really wasn't a happy moment for me. I had anticipated the words coming from Jameson for so long, but they were overshadowed by the words from my doctor. God was playing with me; had to be.

Jameson was busy telling us about the terms of my release. All I heard was I was a free man and that's all I cared about. Morray was smiling, standing up again and rocking Denise in her arms. Me, I was in the bed, just there.

It felt like hours that the conversation was going on and I wasn't able to partake in it. I didn't actually snap out of it until I heard Denise crying. Then I noticed Liana come into the room before anyone else did.

"May we help you?" Morray rolled her neck, still trying to get Denise settled. Liana was looking as if she'd come here expecting a fight. Her hair was pulled up. She wore athletic clothing, and she didn't have on any earrings. She walked right up to Morray and stood in her face.

"Wait, wait. What's going on?" I started to get out of the bed because she was not about to try and fight my wife while she had my daughter in her arms. "Liana why are you even here?"

Her head snapped into my direction as she started to roll her neck. "I'm actually here for you, but your wife decided that she wanted to address me and not stay in a child's position."

Morray started to laugh as she walked away and went to go sit Denise on the sofa. She was now at the age where she could sit up on her own and she was almost ready to start walking. Once her mother sat her down she couch her whining ceased.

"Liana I promise you I'm not the one. I believe I already beat you and your daughter the last time we were all at the hospital together. So you already know this ain't what you want."

My wife stepped back in her face. Jameson grabbed Liana as I

grabbed Morray. Morray was much calmer than I expected. She

wasn't even trying to hit Liana, but still I kept my arms around

her just in case.

A nurse rushed into the room; all late. "Ma'am we are

going to have to ask you to leave. You didn't check in at the front

desk." She pointed to Liana who raised her hand to the nurse and

slapped her. I now see why she and Geneva were together; they

were both crazy.

"I'm not leaving until I've said what I've come here to

say." Liana fixed her clothes and looked at the white nurse who

was holding her face and rushing out of the room to go get help.

"David S. Martin Sr. you are a murderer. You murdered Geneva

and how dare you think you can just get away with that. You

think you are untouchable, but I'm here to tell you that you

aren't." She was now screaming at the top of her lungs.

Two buff male nurses entered the room to get her, but she

was still irate. I had let go of my wife because I realized she was

not the problem. She was chilling, no she was laughing. "This heffa is crazy." Morray went over to the sofa while the men tried handle Liana.

"I promise you I will prove you killed her. He killed my girlfriend; you have to believe me. He's a murderer and God will punish you!" She continued to scream.

Her words weren't affecting me because I knew for a fact that I didn't kill Geneva. I wasn't even a hundred percent sure that she was dead. There was still no physical proof of a body.

The same nurse that Liana had slapped earlier rushed into the room with a syringe and gave Liana something to sedate her. "Get her out of her and place her under psych evaluation. That woman slapped me."

"Do you know this woman?" One of the men asked me as they waited for a gurney. I shook my head *no* and turned my attention back towards Morray.

She was sitting with Denise on her lap, playing with one of the toys she'd brought with her. "You know I'm tired of this right?" She spoke without looking up at me.

I knew she was, but there was nothing much more that I could do. There were plenty of people who were going to suspect me of killing my ex-wife. As long as Morray didn't think I killed her, I was ok.

"Look, I'm going to leave you all to it. Pastor Martin if you need me, just hit my line." Jameson made took his exit, leaving just my family in here.

I went back to sit down on the hospital bed and tried to think of a way to make conversation. Something to get my wife to talk to me more, so I said the first thing that came to my mind. "I don't think she's dead."

My eyes shifted over to my wife, hoping she'd look up at me, and she did. "Hell no she ain't dead. She's like one of those crazy women on *Lifetime*. That woman is over there living a double life somewhere. I just hope she stays her behind over there." She laughed, making me laugh.

"I love you Morray." I bit my bottom lip and tried to soften my face to look *sexy*. We hadn't touched in so long and I was missing the way she made me feel.

"Yea Senior. Those are the words you always tell me."

Chapter Ten

Camille Dumont a.k.a Geneva Martin

Yea, it's me. I know y'all have been reading this book trying to see if I was really dead or not. Hell no I'm not dead. Faking my death was my only option though. I wanted a fresh start. I wanted to get away from all of the hurt that I had caused and start over. So after my fiancé came up with an idea to get us some money from David, I packed my bags.

Of course I could have just left, but it wouldn't have been me if I didn't go out without any drama. So I set the stage and invited David over, telling him that I wanted to speak to him about some things and also apologize for the hurt I caused. By the time he came, I was long gone. I got some human blood from some man that I met online and spread it all over my house.

Now I was here in the French Polynesia, living the life of my dreams. Everything I wanted was at my fingertips and I didn't have to answer to anybody. My life was stress free while I stayed in my home by the ocean.

"So are you going to be ok? I come back in two days, but I don't want you to feel alone." My fiancé was always worried about me being alone in a foreign place, but I was ok. I was a grown woman and I knew how to handle myself.

I climbed out of my bed and walked outside of the double doors that led to the pool area. "Stein, I told you I will be ok baby. I just want you to come back to me." I blew him a kiss through the phone since we were on Facetime. If you were wondering, yes you read that correctly. I said *Stein* as in Mr. Stein, my lawyer.

He technically didn't have to hide out like I did so he was always busy going back and forth, handling business with his firm. Never thought I'd end up with a White man, but here I was engaged to him. I wouldn't actually say I was in love with him, but I really did like him and I enjoyed his company even more. "I'm just saying because I know that area is still new to you."

Stein was so sweet which was something that attracted me to him. He just went with the flow and didn't really challenge me too much. He allowed me to have a strong leading role in our life.

"Babe, I'm fine. Just bring your sexy self back home when you finish this case." I stuck my tongue out being flirtatious.

"I miss you Snuggie," he blew me a kiss. Snuggie was his nickname for me because he said that when we cuddled I was as soft as a snuggie. I didn't get it, but it felt good for someone to actually feel that way about me.

I sat down on the wicker pool chaise and allowed my bronze colored skin to soak up the sun. This little two piece bikini I was wearing was everything. I started holding my phone in different angles to give Stein a show. "You are so beautiful." He always complimented me, and I always smiled like a little high school girl.

"I know, but have you heard anything about my son?" I relaxed and got settled to talk to him some more before I went for my daily swim. It was an amazing thing to be sitting pool side and see a crystal clear ocean at the same time.

Stein sat back in his office chair and took off his glasses allowing me to see his green eyes better. "Actually no I haven't, but Helena and Dean came by today. I was told that your ex-husband was cleared of all charges regarding your case."

I smacked my lips and rolled my eyes because I actually wanted him to do time. "Dang. I wanted him to serve time. So you think they'll close the case?"

"Yes because they don't have any more evidence. It doesn't matter baby because I'm sure they are all suffering from the guilt of how badly they did you before you left."

I had fed Stein a whole bunch of lies about how badly everyone had done me. Down to the fact that Liana tried to kill me, which was the main reason why I needed to get away. Hell it had gotten so easy to lie to him, but I always asked God to forgive me.

"Babe those people need Jesus. I told you that all we have to turn them over to God. They are miserable people and they are letting the devil use them. I told you we are living in the last days." I pushed my short hair out of my face. That was another new thing. I'd cut all of my hair off. I still had a bang, but not a piece of my hair went past my ear.

Stein just looked in the camera and nodded his head.

"Amen, but babe let me go. I'm going to finish this so I can hurry back to my beautiful fiancé and we can finish planning this ceremony." He smirked at me.

I knew he threw that in there because I wasn't rushing to get things in order for our vowel exchange. I didn't see why we needed to do a ceremony. All we needed to do was go to some sort of Justice of the Peace or whatever they had out here. Of course we've made a few friends, but still I didn't think we needed all of that.

"Ok Babe, I will start looking for ministers." I bit my bottom lip. "Talk to you later Stein." I blew him a kiss before I hung up the phone. Now it was time for my day to get started.

****

11 p.m. is when things really got started. The nightlife on the island was to die for. There was something to do differently every night. Tonight I was going to the bar by my lonesome, but I was sure I was going to find someone to occupy my time. Never

did I go too long without company. I didn't even tell my friends

where I was going tonight. I wanted to have fun.

Stepping into the bar in my little sheer white dress with

the spaghetti straps. The bar was really open, very modern.

Everything was white and sleek looking. This bar had a view of

the beach, but it wasn't right on the beach. It was for more of an

upscale crowd.

It was kind of packed today, but that was fine by me. I

took a spot at the bar on the stainless-steel barstool. I gave the

bartender my order of a Henny and Coke before I took out my

phone and started to scroll down my Facebook newsfeed. Even

with this new life I'd made a new profile and all. Everyone knew

me as Camille Dumont a privilege heiress. I'd told everyone that

my grandfather had hit it big in the oil industry, and they actually

believed me. I guess it didn't hurt that the man floating on my

arm was white.

"Cami, I'm surprised to see you here tonight without

Stein. Where is he?" The bartender came back with my drink and

started conversation. I flashed him my million dollar smile before trying out my drink to make sure it was just the right amount of alcohol.

"You know how busy he gets with his cases. So he let me out of the house tonight all by my lonesome." I bit my bottom lip and took in how chiseled his body was. Never before had I noticed the way his muscles bulged out his shirt just a little. He had that athletic build to him.

I guess he caught me looking because he leaned in a little closer. "You know I've always admired your look. Very exotic." This man was doing it for me. He was Black, but his skin was pale and his hair was sandy brown, but he was fine might I add, but did I mention he had an accent. Sounding as if he had to be from South Africa or someplace similar.

Pushing my hair out of my face, I played with my straw as I began to wheel him in. "Well while you've been admiring. You never thought to touch?"

This boy was about half my age; no older than twenty-five, but good Lord he was about to get schooled. Our eyes stayed locked on each other for a few seconds before either of us thought to say anything else. "You know that I've always wanted

to. Are you going to let me?"

Nodding my head, I looked around the room and spotted a

cute blonde waitress in her uniform carrying a bottle of alcohol to

the VIP section. "Yes, but grab her and meet me here once the

bar closes." Quickly I took out a pen from my clutch and began

to write down my address on a napkin.

"I'll see you then." He took the napkin from me once I

was finished and placed it in his back pocket. "Would you like

anything else to drink tonight? All of your drinks will be on the

house."

I stayed in the bar for about another hour or two before I

decided to catch a cab back to my house. The bartender, whose

name happened to be Sebastian, told me just before I left that

they shouldn't be any more than ninety minutes. That was fine by

me because that gave me time to go home and get myself

together. Taking a shower was really what I wanted to do. Not to

mention I wanted to have a little bit more to drink to take the edge off. This would be my first threesome so I was more than

nervous.

By the time the doorbell rang I was waiting in the kitchen

in nothing, but a white see-through robe with nothing underneath,

drinking wine as I sat on the counter. I didn't want to rush to the

door because I didn't want to seem as excited as I was, so I

finished my glass and went.

"I wasn't expecting you all so soon," I lied as I opened

the door. Lord knows I had been watching the clock. Actually,

they were thirty minutes late, but I wasn't going to complain now

that they were here.

Neither one of them responded to my comment as they

made their way inside and we started up the stairs to my

bedroom. "Would you all like something to drink?" I turned

around and looked at them both, but they both shook their heads

no. What in the hell is wrong with them?

Once inside of my master suite, I sat down on the bed. I

wasn't expecting them to just get to it, but once I did take a seat, the girl sat next to me, kissing me on my neck while Sebastian stood in front of me removing his shirt.

"Wait, I don't even know your name Sweetie." I moved my head away from her to look at her. She was a pretty girl, but damn she had to be a whore the way she just started with the sexual encounter without knowing who I was.

"Amelia," she moved closer to me and proceeded to do what she was doing before I stopped her.

This was way more than I was expecting because they both were working on me. The pleasure I was receiving from both of them was giving me this euphoric sensation. My back was laid against the sheets on my bed as Sebastian slid inside of me and Amelia wrote her name with her tongue across my bosom.

My head was going from side to side as my jaw clenched together, trying to hold in my screams. Sebastian was hitting every inch of me and I knew I was already close to opening my dam. Once Amelia moved her tongue, she climbed behind me and held me as I took all the pleasure Sebastian was thrusting.

Her soft kisses on my neck felt nothing like Liana's.

See with Liana it was more love than anything. I can

admit now that I did love her. One could even say I was in love

with her, but I would never say any of this out loud. So sex with

Liana was love making. The entire time the both of us were

proving our love in those long passionate sessions, but here right

now with these two, they just wanted to make me feel good.

Something told me that they both did this on a regular bases.

"Damn Cami, I'm about to bust already." Sebastian

growled as he took his member out of my body and released his

bodily fluid on my abdomen. Before my mind could register that

he'd climaxed, Amelia had already rushed over to lick up the

creamy substance off of my body.

This was amazing. Never had I experienced anything of

this nature. Lord knows that I was already planning on

committing this sin again. I watched her as tongue moved around,

making sure she didn't even leave a drop. My pearl was jumping

just watching her do it.

I laid there in ecstasy, waiting to see what was going to happen next. I just knew it was could only get better from here. The suspicions were confirmed when Sebastian positioned Amelia's body right in front of him and started to give it to her from the back. The most magical part of the entire thing was having Amelia's face between my legs. As rough as Sebastian was going gave her to momentum go work harder on me. If anyone was on the beach at that moment, they heard me screaming. I couldn't hold it in anymore.

I grabbed a hold of Amelia's hair and shoved her closer as I grinded in her face anticipating my climax. "Oh my gosh…" I felt my body go numb as I released everything I had been holding in. That had been my best orgasm since God knows when.

Right as Sebastian was wiping his member off with his shirt, something hit him and he fell to the floor. "What the hell?" I quickly stood up, only to discover Stein standing there holding a bat.

"What is this stuff Geneva? I thought you weren't really gay and here I am witnessing a woman please you while another man is inside of you? This is how you repay me?" He charged at me and wrapped his hand around my throat, dragging me out of the room.

Amelia was screaming, but she dare not say anything. I watched as she stood on the bed, naked, while Stein dragged me further and further away. "Let me go."

How did he even get back? He wasn't supposed to be back tonight or else I would have never done anything like this. I don't know if I feel bad for cheating or because I got caught.

When we finally stopped, we were in the living room. Stein paced around me as I sat on the floor. My back was killing me being that it hit every step on the way down. He must not know who he was dealing with. See me, Geneva, I was not about to allow anyone to try and play me.

I climbed up from the floor, ready to fight. "Who do you think you're playing with? I ain't these White women you are used to." I clapped my hands in his face. He didn't react right away so I stood there and waited for him to do something, but he didn't. "Oh you were so bold a few seconds ago. Dragging me by my throat, but I'm on my feet now and you have nothing to say.

You want to fight? We can fight!"

Stein shook his head and went to sit on the sofa. "No, I'm

not going to fight you because I know that's what you are used

to, but what I will do is make sure to hit you where it hurts."

What in the hell did he mean I was used to that. No I was

not used to being dragged by my throat. Being smacked and

dragged were different things. So I sat down on the sofa on side

of him and waited for him to say something, but he didn't say

anything.

"So what in the world does that mean huh? You think that

I'm some woman that likes getting hit on? Is that what you think

of me? Matter of fact you can leave because I don't need you.

I'm good on my own." Pushing myself up from my seat I decided

to leave and go back to the room to make sure Sebastian and

Amelia were ok.

The house was eerie quiet which was strange because

although I was used to being alone, it was ok for it to be quiet

then, but when there are four people in a house you would think that there would be some sort of talking or noise making going on, but here you could hear a pen drop.

Amelia was standing over Sebastian when I got back to the room trying to make sure that he was ok. He held his head and he was bleeding profusely. "Hey you need to get him to a hospital. He's bleeding on my floors." I screamed and ran to get a towel to help them.

They both looked at me shocked. I don't know what they expected from me, but as far as I was concerned I didn't know them and I had enough problems in my life because of them. "How are we supposed to get there? I don't know how to drive and he drove us here." Amelia cried out as she wrapped the towel I had given her around his head. Sebastian's eyes were starting to close and I was getting scared. I couldn't be responsible for a death of a man that I barely even knew.

"I don't know, but you have to get him out of here before he dies Sweetheart." I rushed to find his keys and his clothes before I threw it at her. Sebastian's eyes started to open back up again, but they were low. Hell, he was not about to die in my house and hunt me. So, I helped her pick him up. "I'll help you get him to the car, but after that you all are on her own."

This man was a whole lot bigger than what I had expected. Getting him off the floor was like pulling an elephant up by its nose. Sebastian could barely keep his head straight. Once we made it to the door, his head landed on my shoulder and I could feel his blood running down my back. My skin was crawling because I was scared he had AIDs and I was going to get it.

Amelia unlocked the doors to his Opel Astra which were quite popular on the island. "Open the back door." I urged her because we were both struggling to hold up this horse of a man. I was stumbling down the driveway. Sebastian started to mumble something, but his words fell on deaf ears.

"What am I supposed to do now?" Amelia whined once we pushed him into the car, not bothering to even make sure he was comfortable. I threw the towel in the back seat with him, but I felt so disgusted that I turned my back and started to walk away as Amelia kept talking. They were out of my house so they were

no longer my problem.

I was still naked and being that my closest neighbors were

almost a half of a mile away, it didn't bother me. What did bother

me was having someone else's bodily fluid on my skin. Stein was

standing in the doorway waiting for me when I back to the house.

"I thought you weren't gay?"

"Look I don't have time for your jokes right now.

Someone is about to die and they bled on me. We need to be

praying for that young man that you almost killed. You can go to

jail for that." I side-eyed him and stepped around him so that I

can head back to the bedroom.

Stein followed behind me every step I took. I was still

upset with him, but I figured that he was more upset with me.

Yes, I did cheat, but can you blame me? Ask yourself this

question: if you were on a beautiful island all alone while your

fiancé was thousands of miles of way, wouldn't you do what I

did? Technically I didn't commit any sins. The commandment

says that thou shalt not commit adultery and you must be married

for that.

"It's amazing to me how evil you truly are. When I first

met you, I thought the little plan to send your husband to jail for

your murder was cute, but now I realize it is sick because you

don't understand when enough is enough. As to think that I loved

you. Wow Geneva, you had me fooled, but I guess that you're

just like the rest of *those* people." Stein's words didn't affect me

in the slightest. I knew he was trying to throw daggers at my race,

but it was funny to me so I continued to go about fixing my water

for my shower.

Stein stood right there by the sink and watched me. I

didn't understand why he was still here. If he was that hurt, he

would have left long before we even got Sebastian in that car. I

kept my eye on him as I placed my body under the steaming hot

water. *White ass*, I laughed to myself.

"It's funny that you are trying to be funny about my race,

Stein, but don't you people sleep with your own fathers and

brothers? I heard that you people even have sex with the sheep and chickens. Please don't get me started on you people, and why are you still here? Did I not tell you to leave?" I poured some of my soap on to my puff and started to lather my body so that I could turn him on. I knew him and I knew he was just as into sex as I was.

My fiancé, or ex-fiancé, bit his bottom lip as he watched me. I'm sure he was trying to speak, but his physical capabilities was overpowering his mental capabilities. I kept my eyes on him as I rubbed the soap all over my body while making sure to go extra slow so that he could keep up. It literally took me about five minutes to get every part of my body, and yes I do mean every part including my hair. Once I was done, I rinsed myself off and turned off the water.

I grabbed the towel off the hook and waltzed into the bedroom dripping wet because I already knew what was going to take place. Yes, of course Stein was going to make love to me and make me remember why I got with him in the first place. He made me even regret that I had even done that to him. He worked my body out in more ways than a Planet Fitness ever could.

The Other Side Of The Pastor's Bed 3

When we went to sleep, I had asked God to forgive me for all the

sins I had committed and that he helped me right my wrongs.

What I wasn't expecting was to wake up to find my bed and bank

account empty.

Chapter Eleven

First Lady Morray

Although I told David that I loved him, it still felt good to have my family back together again. My husband was home and yes he was dealing with his recent diagnosis, but still he was in good spirits. He was even better with Denise than he was before he left. It felt good to have him wrap his arms around me as I slept. I loved him, but I was in love with David. Nonetheless, I was going to do right by my husband.

"So she usually sleeps like this? Are you sure she's comfortable?" Senior laid on his side with his hand propping up his head as we both watched Denise lay deep asleep while she held her right foot in her left hand. I don't know why she did it, but she'd been doing it for a few months now.

I shook my head and continued to watch my baby girl peacefully rest. Senior reached over Denise and took my hand into his and brought it up to his mouth. I was confused as to what he was doing, but I didn't stop him. He stared at me and smiled.

"Baby I thank God for placing such a strong woman by my side. I couldn't have done any of this without you. I love you more than life itself and even when you think I'm just doing things because my flesh is getting the best of me, remember I do everything for you and Denise."

His words were so sweet, but it made me question him. What would his flesh be doing that I needed to remember that he loved me? He should know that I'm not the type of woman you can just tell stuff to.

"Yea Senior. We love you too." I half smiled, but I tried my best to keep my insecurities to myself. I'll always remember that Senior cheated on his last wife with me so who was I to think that he wouldn't cheat on me. Only a fool would even let a thought like that come across their mind.

Slowly, I pulled my hand back from my husband and adjusted myself in the bed being careful not to disturb Denise. It was almost eleven at night and I knew I was going to be swamped the next morning because I wanted to get a head start on planning Denise's christening and I was going all out. Sparing no expense because I also going to celebrate my one year

wedding anniversary.

"You think we could have another child?" Senior's words

alerted me and almost made me forget how sleepy I was. Maybe

before I wanted more children with him, but as of now Denise

was all we were going to have.

Trying to choose my words carefully I bit my lip. "We'll

see. Let's just worry about making sure you are ok first. With the

cancer and all, we need to take care of you." I smiled so that he

wouldn't realize how bothered I was by his question.

Senior didn't say anything else and I kissed my baby girl

before I closed my eyes. My body must have been more tired

than I thought because I don't even recall going to sleep. I just

recall waking up in the middle of the night to go to use the toilet

and my husband wasn't in our bed.

This nigga must have lost his entire mind in jail because it

was one-thirty in the morning and he was nowhere inside of our

home. I looked, I checked, and I even doubled checked to make

sure because I didn't want to be right. This man had strayed from

out of our bed this late. My grandmother always said that nothing

was open past ten o'clock, but legs and clubs. Being that my

Senior was married and a pastor, he didn't need to be in either.

Thankfully, I had recently installed a tracking device on

his car. Yes, I was that desperate. Rushing over to my phone, I

opened the app and used my thumbprint to access the

information. I wanted so desperately to believe that he'd gone to

the church or even to the hospital, but when his location told me

neither place, but across town, my heart started to beat fast

because I just knew what was going one. Still I needed to see for

myself. I had to.

Calling the only two people I knew would help me go

find my husband, I started dressing myself and moved Denise

into the bassinet. No I wasn't going to bring her with me, but

somebody was going to have to watch her.

"Well I'll just come over there and sit with her while you

and Helena go check. I can't believe this man." Kedra yawned

into the phone.

Kayla Andrè

I took my bonnet off my head and quickly grabbed my hair to place it into a bun on top of my head. I was dressed to fight my husband. Wasn't too worried about whoever he was with because she didn't owe me any loyalty. Adidas tracksuit and tennis shoes.

"I don't know why you are surprised. We've always known he wasn't too much, but it's ok we are going to go get him tonight. I'm already on my way Morray." Helena was more amped than I was. I didn't know what was going to happen tonight, but God just don't let it get too crazy.

Helena and I rolled in silence as she listened carefully to Siri direct us to my husband's location. Since hardly anyone was on the road, it took us about twenty minutes to pull up. Helena turned her lights off and parked across the street from the lime green townhome.

"Whoever this heffa is, I already know she has horrible taste." Helena sat back in her seat and we watched the house. No lights were on, but my husband's Bentley was parked in the driveway. No discretion at all, but he swore he loved me.

The butterflies were taking over because I became so nervous about the entire situation. When I saw the car in the driveway that made the entire situation surreal. Before my mind could think of what I wanted to do next, Helena opened her door and got out of the car. "What are you doing girl?" I jumped out of the car and started to chase her. She headed for the backyard. "Helena I know you aren't thinking what I think you are thinking." I grabbed her arm to stop her.

We were whispering, but I still felt as though someone could hear me. Then on top of that she was thinking of breaking into someone's home. My husband just got home from prison and I was not trying to go in his place. A light came on in the neighbor's home. Helena nodded her head at me.

"Morray we are going to make sure that your husband is doing what we think he is doing. Now come on most people in Florida have a screened in patio and they never lock that door and that also means that lock the door that leads from the house to the patio." Helena jerked her arm away from me and continued to walk.

Saying a quick prayer to God, that He would not allow us to get caught, I followed behind her. Just like she said, the door was unlocked and then the door to the house was unlocked. All the lights were off in the living room, but the light on in the stairwell was on. From what I could see was the house was nice. Yes, I was checking out the house. I couldn't see the paint I on the walls, but the house seemed to have a modern flow to it.

Helena waited by the stairs for me to lead. I looked back at her before I started, thinking that maybe we should turn around. "Oh my gosh Morray if you don't just go." She shoved me up the stairs. It made a small thump. I held my breath because I thought we'd been caught, but there was nothing. Instead of screams of fear that a robber was in the home, we heard a loud cry of pleasure.

With my anger fueling me, I didn't even need Helena anymore. I was ready to catch my husband in the act. I tipped toed up the stairs and followed the sounds of the moans to a door at the end of the upstairs hallway. My heart was beating fast and

I'm sure under my arms were sweating and sure was the crack of

my behind, but I couldn't stop.

The closer I got the more my head started to pound and I

was sure I wasn't seeing anything clearly. The lights in the room

were off, but there was a light coming from somewhere. I didn't

know if it was the bathroom light or a light coming from the

closet, but it was just the right amount for me to see. The door

was slightly ajar so I pushed it ever so slightly.

Before I could scream, Helena's hand wrapped around my

mouth as we stood in the doorway and watched my husband

make love to his mistress. The way they lay in the missionary

position with his face laying in her neck with one hand on her

thigh broke my soul. Each thrust he made inside of her she let out

a loud moan. I heard his breaths too, and they were so into it that

neither of them realized that they were being watched.

I couldn't stop the tears, but I couldn't blame anyone, but

myself because this was my fault. This was karma. I deserved

this, but it didn't make it hurt any less. Yes, I did sleep with a father and his son, but I was married and I was now watching my husband love on another woman.

This was all too much to take in. I shook my head and turned around to leave. I didn't even bother to be quiet. I just walked out of the house and made my way back to Helena's vehicle.

"I'm sorry Morray. I knew what we were going to find, but somewhere in the back of my mind I thought we could be wrong." Helena began to apologize, but I held my hand up to stop her.

I didn't want to talk. I didn't need her apologizes or even *I told you so's*. I just wanted to sit with the thoughts in my head and figure out my next move. I was heartbroken, but was I ready to be done with my husband? There was one thing I was certain about. Things were about to change for the Martin household.

Chapter Twelve

Pastor David

"Mo, you think maybe this weekend we can take Denise to Lowry Park? She's never been to the zoo and I'm thinking that since I'm home now and with everything going on we can have some family time." I walked into the kitchen where my wife was sitting at the breakfast table feeding Denise. "Bae you heard me?" I questioned her when she didn't respond to me.

I got my water out of the fridge and waited for an answer, but she still didn't say anything by the time I closed the refrigerator door. "Mo." I walked up to the side of the highchair. Denise turned to look at me with a mouth full of mashed potatoes, but she still smiled revealing her two bottom teeth.

"What do you want David?" She slammed the bowl of mashed potatoes down so hard on the glass table that a little landed on the outside of the bowl. For the past two days, she's been walking around here with this big attitude and not to mention she's been sleeping in a guest room with Denise saying

that she has a cold.

Not wanting to argue much in front of my daughter, I just

turned around and walked away. I didn't know what was wrong

with my wife, but something was up. She probably was cheating

on me. I knew damn well she didn't know about my dealings

with Miranda because I made sure to cover all my tracks. I only

go late at night and then Miranda lives across town.

By the time I hit the stairs, I decided that I did want to let

my wife know how unhappy I am. This was getting ridiculous. I

was a man with cancer. She needed to respect me. "Look Morray,

I am your husband and you will respect me. I do everything for

you and Denise to make sure that you don't even have to lift a

finger. One would think that my wife would at least respond back

to me when I ask her a question. It's fine because as the head of

the family, I'm letting you know that we are going to the zoo this

weekend. So, cancel any plans that you may have. We are also

going to church on Sunday as a family and then to the zoo!"

I made sure to put some bass in my voice so she could tell that I was not playing with her. She was going to respect me. I had been away too long so she probably forgot how things worked in this house, but I would get her back in check in no time. I have no time for someone to disrespect me and I'm putting food in their mouths and clothes on their back.

Once my speech was done, I waited for my wife to respond to me. She didn't seem to be phased at all. "Are you done?" She slapped her thighs and looked up at me. I took a moment to think if I was done and then nodded my head.

Morray handed Denise her cup and stood up from her chair. "David I don't care about any of this." She took her finger and twirled it in the air letting me know she was talking about the house and my money. "I'm here for you, but it's you that isn't appreciative of what you have. You must think I'm stupid, don't you? Look, just leave me the hell alone. Don't talk to me right now because I'm ready to slit your throat. Take care of Denise. I'll be back whenever."

Morray grabbed her phone off the table, kissed Denise, and left. Well that didn't go the way I expected to go at all. I was left dumbfounded, standing there as Denise watched me with her juice cup in her hand. She took the cup out her mouth and smiled. "Ma," she cheered.

This was the first time I ever heard her say anything close to a real word. As excited as I was, I couldn't fully express it because her *Ma* had pissed me off. On top of that, what could she think I thought she was stupid for? I haven't said or done anything to feel as such.

"I'm Daddy Denise. Your mommy went bye-bye." I went to pick her up, and she just giggled and drooled as if what I said was amusing to her. As if she knew her mother wouldn't leave her.

As I was coming out of the kitchen, I saw Morray heading out the door before she slammed it. "Ma," Denise cheered again. Hell, she was never that excited about me.

Since it would be just she and I today, I decided that we'll chill and watch *Belly*, one of my favorite movies. I liked what it represented. Sincere and Buns both had significance. Sincere

reminded me of myself although Buns and I had things in

common as well. Not even thirty minutes into the movie, my

phone started to ring. Looking down at the screen, I saw it was

my mother who doesn't usually call me, but of course Denise

thought it was her mother.

"Hello Mother?"

"I'm outside Son," was all she said before she hung up the

phone.

My mother never was one to even come by my house.

Even when I was with Geneva my mother didn't come by. We

weren't what you considered close. Never were. When I was

younger my parents sent me off to boarding school. It wasn't just

me, but my other three siblings as well. She was a mother of four

boys and all of them had boys, but I was the only one to have a

daughter, giving me the keys to the kingdom.

Before I opened the door for her, I had to make sure

Denise was up to par, but I should have known that she would be.

Morray had this girl dressed up every day as if she were going somewhere important.

"Hello Mother, what brings you by?" I stepped to the side while she let herself into my home, looking around trying to see. She held her clutch purse close to her and her nose up in the air.

Once she made her way to the formal living area, she sat down on the sofa and crossed her ankles. She sat her purse down to the side and reached for Denise. "Hand me my grandbaby and go get me some water. I would prefer sparkling water."

I didn't know the cause of my mother's surprise visit, but I was sure to find out. When I returned from the kitchen with a bottle of Voss water and a cup of ice her eyebrows rose as she shook her head. "We are out of sparkling water." I apologized.

"I won't show my behind because I like Morray more than I ever cared for Geneva." She spoke to Denise in such a cheerful voice as if she was saying something positive. Well I guess in a way she was.

Since my mother was going to play around, I just sat down in the chair across from her and waited for her to begin.

She sat Denise on her lap facing forward before pouring the water into her glass and taking a sip. "Well I'm sure you know why I'm here." She sat the glass back down and patted Denise's thigh.

"Well honestly, Mother, I do not. You never come by. Not without at least calling first." I rubbed my hands across my thigh because my hands were clamming up. No matter how old I got I knew my mother had the power crush me.

She turned Denise around to face her as she cooed in her face. Denise was smiling, but I doubt she actually knew who my mother was. "Now that you have this beautiful princess you oversee this family, but I am not liking the direction everything is going. Your uncle was doing a fine job by this family. Troy tells me that some money has come up missing. I swear on your children's life, if you don't get us back on track it will be you and I."

Craziest thing was the entire time she was talking, she was cooing. Smiling and talking with Denise, but spoke of death. My daughter didn't even understand the danger she was in.

"Mother the family is fine. I was just locked away, but we will be good." I assured her and fixed my posture in the chair to let her know that I was serious about my words.

Elma Martin was eighty-seven years old and had probably one nice bone in her body. "What's up with the hospital? I haven't heard anything about it."

"Jameson finished all of the paperwork. It's a go." I got up out of the chair and stood up. I was becoming more and more uncomfortable by the minute.

My mother chuckled to herself about me. "Sit down Son. Acting like a common criminal. I know I've taught you better than the work you are showing me. The membership at the church is down by two thousand members now. My poor husband is turning in his grave. I know he is."

Now that was funny. My father was a worse man than I was. He had mistress living in a house that the church owned, but that wasn't my place to remind my mother. If she wanted to forget some key points in her life to make her sleep at night, then I guess I could pretend as well.

"Well I need for you to get it together and do some damage control. Your daughter gave you the power to damn near control this entire state so do something with it. Now we have the paperwork together we can start the operation as well." She placed Denise down on side of her and started to pick up her glass. "I was told that with more people getting killed. The Black Market is booming and I want to claim our steak."

I nodded my head and walked around to pick up Denise. Having my daughter in my hands made me wish that she never encountered people like us, but who was I kidding? She was going to be a person like us. She had no choice, especially because she was going to be trained in this business.

"I will mother, but I've been busy dealing with life. I was diagnosed with lung cancer. I've been dealing with that and not to mention I was just released from prison." I sat back down in my chair with Denise in my lap. Her hands started to play with the collar of my shirt. She smiled at me when I brought my eyes down upon hers.

My mother took another sip of her glass before she said

something else. "Son, those are personal issues that you must

deal with on your own. My concerns are about the family. I don't

have too many years left on this Earth so I would like to continue

to live the lifestyle that I've grown accustom too."

Elma spoke like the witch I knew her to be. Having lung

cancer was nothing to her. Her biggest concern was making sure

that she could fly to Dubai when she pleased. Her parents raised

her on the money they made from the Black Market. At first it

was just dealing with the staff and paying them off to get some

body's so they could sell the body parts across seas. Now we've

secured the required documents we needed to start our own

hospital.

"Ok Mother. Is that all you needed?" By now I was ready

for her to go. She'd been here long enough and her welcome was

over a few minutes ago. "I'm about to lay Denise down for her

nap."

"Son, I'll leave you be, but I will keep my eye out on you.

Your brother is flying to Cuba tomorrow to meet with some

buyers. I would appreciate if you could do anoth

drive at the church." She pulled herself up from the so

and grabbed her purse. I got up to walk her out, but didn't reall

want to so I just followed behind her to the door.

Once my mother left, I went back to the living room. Denise wasn't going to fall asleep, which I knew. I just wanted to get my mother out of the house. Even with me being as messed up as I am, I still didn't know about everything my family had going on. Don't get me wrong, we made great money doing what we did, but now I was starting to feel like I wanted to get right with God since I was this close to death.

Chapter Thirteen

David Jr.

nce my father was back in the picture, things between Morray and I were back to where they were after I first found out they were messing around on me. Sometimes she would call me, but most of the time she would be trying to get her family together. That hurt me, but I should have known it would be too good to be true. I was just a convenience to Morray, so I came back to Markia.

She'd decided to transfer to a school out here in Tampa and had gotten an apartment so I decided to stay with her since Hannah was breathing down my back about being together. Markia and I were just cool, but we went to sleep in the same bed and occasionally had sex.

"So how do you like living with me?" Kia was standing at the stove making something for dinner.

"It's cool and all." I shrugged my shoulders and con.

to wash the dishes. Since I was staying here rent free, I though.

the least I could do was clean the dishes I ate off.

That's another thing about staying here. I didn't have to

pay for anything. I didn't even have to buy groceries. Kia's

apartment was covered by the school because of her GPA and she

received Food Stamps. So, there was nothing for me to spend my

money on, but me and I was fine with that.

"I meant with us being around each other so much. I

missed you while we were apart, but I don't know if you missed

me much."

Trying to stop myself from laughing in her face, I let out a

cough. Being with her was the last thing on my mind when I

wasn't by her. The reason I'm here now is because I needed a

place to stay while school was out. "Yea, I did."

That lie made Kia so happy. She threw the spoon down

she was using to stir the pot and ran over to hug me. "I know

babe. I'm just excited we are back together. I know I said a lot of out of line, but I am here now and I want to say that I am

y."

I couldn't even think of some words to say because I knew whatever I did say would be a lie. Turning the water off, I took a deep breath before I turned around and hugged her back. I was going to keep this going until I had somewhere else to lay my head.

"I'm glad too, but you know I'm not really with the touchy feelings type of stuff." I hugged her with one arm while keeping the other one by my side. Kia reached up to get a kiss, so I gave her one. I figured I'd go even further and try to get some sex out of it.

Kia's body was like my playground. She aimed to please me during sex, so I knew once I slid my tongue in her mouth, my message would get across. Once she took heed to my advance, I picked her up and walked us to the room. Throwing her on the bed, I went to get a condom out of the nightstand drawer before taking off my clothes.

The Other Side Of The Pastor's Bed 3

By the time I got back to the bed, Kia was on a[ll fours?]

behind in the air, waiting on Daddy to slide in. Passing my [hand?]

over her slit first to see how wet she was, I was slightly surpr[ised]

that she was dripping. "Damn. You really missed me?"

"Waiting for you to come back to me."

With her walls gripping my shaft, I started to work up a

rhythm. I knew I wanted to get off, but for some reason I felt like

I had a point I needed to prove to her. I wanted her to always be

in love with me, even if I wasn't in love with her. She needed to

long for me like I longed for Morray.

Placing my hands on both sides of her hips, I began to

drill her. Going as fast as I could. This wasn't the time for love

making. It was time for her to get screwed. It didn't take long

before I felt her insides become tighter as she tried to lock me in.

"Yea, you like that huh? Tell Daddy you love him." I

moved one hand to her hair to pull it. I knew I was working her.

"I love you Daddy, I love you. My gosh," she started to

hiss through her teeth.

ore she could get a chance to release herself, I forced

rn around. I wanted to get in from the front too because I

v she loved that. With her knees up by her shoulder, I picked

1y speed back up. I wanted her to feel it, and I knew she was.

The way she was turning her head from side to side, hands

gripping the sheets, I was for sure I was beating it up.

Hell, I was going so hard that I couldn't hold back

anymore. I was about to release myself. "Let go in my mouth,"

Kia demanded. All she had to tell me was one time because I

pulled out of her and snatched this latex off in an instant. Her lips

wrapped around my member and I let my whole life go.

I couldn't see straight so I sat down on the end of the bed

until my head stopped spinning. Sitting up wasn't doing any

justice so I laid down. Kia got in between my legs and started to

massage my member. "I don't know what it is about you that

makes me crazy in love with you, but I don't want this feeling to

go away."

As she spoke, I thought about getting back inside of her

for another round. All her love talk was too much for me. Sitting back up in the bed, I looked down at her as she looked up at me still massaging me. Kia was so beautiful and I started to feel like my father again. Messing over women who actually cared about me, but it was as if I couldn't stop the things I did. This was who I was, who I was meant to be.

"David Samuel Martin Jr., will you do me the honor of becoming my husband?" She then proceeded to suck me off, leaving me dumbfounded. I didn't know if I needed to curse her out or pat her back for doing a good job.

There was no way I was going to say yes to a marriage proposal. Especially when I knew deep down who I wanted to be with. I wasn't marrying anyone else if it wasn't for Morray. I wasn't that horrible to marry her just because while already knowing that I would never love her the way she loved me.

"Nah, wait Kia." I gently pushed her away from me and got up from the bed. "I'm sorry Kia, but I can't do this."

"What do you mean you can't do this? I'm down here sucking you dry and you can't do this? You don't want to marry me?" Kia got up from her knees to face me.

I started to put my clothes back on. Damn, it seemed like very woman I tried to talk to wanted more than I was willing to give. This was one of the many reasons why I loved Morray. We had our own pace and weren't trying to rush anything.

"Can you tell me why you don't want to marry me?" She came closer to me, snatching my shirt out of my hand. I could walk around shirtless, that was fine by me. "Come on DJ, tell me."

There was a hard knock at the door. "Go answer the door and we'll talk about it. It's not you.; it's me."

"Wow, this BS of a line is what you are going to give me? The woman that is taking care of you? Your ride or die?"

Was she trying to be comical because her telling me that she was my ride or die was one of the funniest things I've heard in a long time. I sat back down on the bed in my jeans and shoes on. I wanted to get out of here before we got into a big fight. I didn't want there to be bad blood between us, but she wasn't giving me an option. The knock at the door became harder, and for some reason it was bothering me. I got up to go get it.

"I asked you to go get the door. We can talk about it afterwards." I reached out to open the front door, but Kia came, damn near knocking me over to answer the door. It was a damn shame because she still was naked.

I started to walk away as she opened the door, trying to stand behind it while keeping only her head and shoulder visible. "What in the hell are you doing at my house," Kia screamed causing me to look back over my shoulder.

Damn how does shawty keep poppin' up like this? "Yea, is David home?" Morray spoke confidently. As if she wasn't coming to another woman's house to ask for me.

"Yea, I'm here." I walked back over to the door. By passing Kia to get outside where Morray was. I knew my girl was back for me.

Chapter Fourteen

First Lady Morray

After I left the house, I didn't know where to go. I knew I needed to get out of there. I wasn't ready to tell him that I knew he was stepping out on our marriage because honestly, I didn't know what I was going to do. Letting him in on my secret meant that I needed to have everything in line. If I was going to leave this marriage, I needed to be sure. Thankfully, I'd been stashing some money since the beginning of our marriage because I knew he was going to do something like this.

David had texted me a few days ago to let me know that he'd been staying with Markia at her new apartment; even sent me the address. Going there to be disrespectful wasn't my intention, but I needed David right now. Helena and Kedra were both busy with their families and I felt bad for having them out late the other night.

"So what did you come here for?" David came and rested his back against my car, pulling a gar wrapper from his pocket.

That was one thing I don't think he'll ever stop doing, but he needs too because I know the football team drug tests. "You want to hit this?"

Nodding my head, I watched as he placed the blunt between his full pink lips and fired it up. My mind wondered back to the many times we used to lay in my bed at my old home and pass the blunt between the both of us, telling stories of how life would be when we could be public after his eighteenth birthday. I guess God had jokes.

I was so wrapped up in my own brain that I didn't even notice David's hand out in front of me. "Huh," he brought it up to my eyes for me to see.

"My bad, but I just wanted to talk to you. Things are getting crazy and I don't know what to do." David wrapped his arm around my shoulders as I snuggled closer to him. I was sure Markia was looking out the window at us. I took a pull of the blunt, trying to look back and see if I could see her, but I couldn't.

"Well what's wrong? I know Denise is ok because if she wasn't you wouldn't be here." He laughed, taking the blunt from me. Honestly, I was comfortable telling him the problems of my marriage because he was my best friend, still.

"Your father is cheating on me and I don't know what to do."

"What you thought he would be faithful to you? I know you have to be smarter than that Morray." He laughed at me, but I didn't care.

I moved away from him a little, just to look back up at him. "David this isn't funny. This is my life."

"And it was my life when you decided that it'll be ok to sleep with my father no matter what the blackmail would have been, I thought we were better than that." David brought the blunt up to his lips to take another puff, but he gazed deep into my eyes and I knew he was still hurt.

There was no reason for me to try to defend myself because he will always be allowed to speak his truth. If that's what he was still feeling, then that's what it was. "I'm sorry, but

I'm just done with everything. I'm seriously thinking about leaving."

David stepped back to look at me. "You serious?" He thought I was playing, but I was dead serious. "If you serious we can do this thing."

"I'm serious David. I'm ready to divorce your father. I even met up with someone to discuss my options." Senior and I should have never been together, but since we did end up married I needed to know what would happen to me if I were to leave.

David grabbed me by my waist and pulled me closer to him. "You ever stopped loving me?" He looked down at me and placed the blunt to my lips for me to take a puff before he put it out.

After I exhaled the smoke, I reached up and kissed his lips. "No and I never will." It felt good to be back in his arms and though neither of us said it, I knew this was the beginning of us again.

"I've always loved you too. Even with everything, you'll always be my queen. Although it hurts, I do forgive you. Just don't do me like that again." He pecked my lips again. "Aye,

follow me somewhere." The smile that was on my face was

probably able to be spotted from miles away. I knew I was

beaming because I had my man back. The love of my life and the

person that I never stopped loving, still loved me.

Although I didn't know where we were going, I followed

behind him in my car. We ended up a few miles away from

where we were standing to a row of townhomes. David whipped

his charger into the driveway and parked. Not know whose house

we were at, I parked of the street.

"You like it?"

I walked up to him and looked around. Since he said it

like that, I knew this was his place, but I was trying to understand

how he could afford this and why would he get a place here in

Tampa knowing that he has to go back to Miami. The place was

seriously nice.

"How could you afford this?" I stood behind him while he

unlocked the door. He turned around swiftly and scooped me up before I had a chance to protest. "Put me down," I screamed at him, but I really didn't want him to.

The house was even nicer on the inside. The butter cream colored wall and wood floors led the way to the immaculate living quarters. The stairs were right by the door on the right-hand side with living room entrance on the left. There was crème and black furniture with nice decorations. It was obvious that he didn't decorate this himself.

"You like it?" He sat me down on the kitchen island which was white marble. I glanced around the room before I answered him. There was even a dining table with five chairs that accompanied it.

"Babe this is nice, but I need you to tell how you are affording this." I wiped my hands over his shirt. His V-neck shirt was showing all his physique.

"Well, Andre's family had this place and they couldn't find a renter nor did Andre want to stay here, so they told me I could. Six months free. I could've been moved in, but it was cool living for free by Kia." He spoke with his hands up in the air,

overly excited.

Pulling him close to me, I kissed his lips. "That's

beautiful Baby. Well how is everything with school?"

"Well everything with school isn't what I want it to be,

but I got called in to try out of the Dodgers?" His words weren't

coming across clear to me because Dodgers were a baseball team

and this man was going to Miami on a football scholarship. I

pushed him back some so he could see my confused facial

expression. "Before you came to school, I was on the baseball

team, but I wasn't sure if I liked it or not. Then the other day

while I was visiting Steven he had his friend over who was a

scout for the Dodgers. Long story short, we showed him some

tapes and he invited me out to play."

"God," was all I could say. God had been putting and

work and preformed a miracle. "Babe that is amazing!"

"You want to know what else is amazing?" He licked his

lips and started to kiss on my neck. My womanhood was

throbbing and I knew what was sure to follow this moment.

I moved his head over so our lips could meet. Clothes started to come off, and before we knew it we were on the kitchen floor. Passionately making love. We looked in each other's eyes the entire time. The love that overcame me, allowed me to keep climaxing. Once I felt like he'd done enough for me, I flipped us over to show him what I could do for him. Riding him until his eyes rolled to the back of his head was the plan, and I accomplished it.

We even headed upstairs to break in his master bedroom. It was a beautiful escape for the reality I was facing. Also, it made me feel good to be getting back at my husband, but the best thing about the entire experience was remembering how much I loved David.

"You know if you are serious about leaving my father, you and Denise are more than welcome over here." His words baffled me because I didn't know if he was serious. "Yes, I'm serious. You can move in whenever you'd like."

He started to rub his hand up my thigh and over to my honey pot until one finger was in front of me. "You want to live with me?" With his fingers working my insides I was too focused

to answer him, but I already knew the answer. Home is where the

heart is, so my home was wherever David was.

Chapter Fifteen

Pastor David

With everything going on I wasn't paying much attention to the church. The amount we usually took in each week from collection had gone down. We were used to making twenty-thousand dollar deposits every Monday, but the last drop was only eight grand. The youth department decided to host a car was to earn money for their group. So, as the leader of the church I came to help them wash cars to make sure that the community knew I was back. After a while, I felt warn out so I went to sit down on the bench next to Troy.

"How does it feel being home with Morray and the baby?" Troy was busy on his phone, like always. I appreciated him though because he kept all of my family's finances together. He's a certified accountant, but he had his hand in so many different business deals that I was sure put him in the top one percent.

"She hasn't been herself since I got back. Well I mean when I first got back she was fine, but now she's distant. Doesn't respond to me when I speak to her nor does she even want to be in the same room with me." Morray had even been acting worse than that. The past few nights she hasn't stayed at the house and she says it's because Helena had just had some fertility surgery and she was helping her out, but I was sure that was a lie.

Troy put away his phone and looked over at me. "Man, you gotta stop doing this. I never get in your personal business, but honestly David we're getting too old for these streets. Besides they did tell you that you had cancer. Whatever you got going on with that woman needs to stop. Morray has been doing really well handling this situation, but I'm sure even she has her breaking point. This ain't Geneva you're dealing with. Not to mention adding Miranda to your entire situation."

Why was it that every time I spoke about my wife to someone they wanted to remind me that she wasn't like Geneva, but that was something I already knew. Morray was the exact opposite of Geneva and that's what I loved about her. Another thing was the fact that she showed me that she was down for me.

She honestly had a chance to divorce me while I was in prison, but she never even mentioned it.

"Yea, I know who I'm married to. You don't understand, Brother. That woman got me out of jail. I owe her."

"There was no evidence to even keep you in there. Eventually you would have gotten out. You want to continue sleeping with Miranda. Just admit that and stop acting as if you're only doing it for that specific reason. Man, I've been knowing you since we were kids; you can't lie to me."

This conversation with Troy was starting to stress me out. I didn't want to think about the wrong I was doing in my relationship. I had too much to think about with the church and now the hospital that my family has decided to acquire, and everyone was forgetting that I was a walking cancer patient.

Thinking about the hospital made me remember that I needed Troy to handle something. "Did we get the mayor to sign-off on that thing we talked about?"

Troy picked back up his phone and started back with whatever he was doing beforehand. "Yea, but you know that can't be in writing on either side so it's a verbal agreement, but yes. We have all our required staff and we secured some captains who are willing to transport double the amount of bodies we will have on hand."

That's all I needed to hear. More bodies meant more money. With my mother willing to take my power away from me, I needed to ensure that I would replace the money that I was sure Geneva stole when she faked her own death, but she'd have to deal with God about that,

After I left from the carwash, I stopped by Godiva Chocolatier and picked up Mo's favorite truffles and a dozen white chocolate covered strawberries, and then headed to her favorite flower shop and picked up some roses. I knew I needed to treat my wife better and I had made up in my mind that soon I would end my affair with Miranda, but I don't know exactly when.

Sex with her was good, and easy. It was an escape from everything that I had going in my life. I haven't tried to think much about the cancer, but I knew it was there. Nobody wanted to focus on a death sentence. As a pastor, you'd expect me to talk to God about it, but I had so many other things that I wanted God to handle first that I figured that I could just deal with this one on my own.

Turning my car onto to my street, I spotted two massive moving trucks pulling out of my driveway. *What the hell?* I thought to myself. If this woman had moved the things my money paid for out of my house because she wanted to leave me, she had another thing coming.

I pressed down on the gas pedal and speed past the trucks to cut them off at the end of the street. They came to a screeching halt, almost hitting each other. I knew they weren't trying to hit this Bentley.

Once they stopped, I hopped out my car as some Mexican man hopped down from the driver's side of the first truck. "My friend, what are you doing? Are you crazy? We could've hit you."

"Why are you taking stuff from my house? Where in the hell are you going with all of my stuff?" My blood was boiling because how could this wench try and take my stuff and leave me. "Bring all that back to my house. Right now," I pointed my finger back towards my house, but this lil wet back laughed at me.

"I cannot do that, Sir. I have a signed contract by the person who orchestrated this move. The only way we'd be allow to return the things to this house is if they allowed us." He stood with his hands on his hips nonchalant. Some of his amigos got out of the trucks and headed over our way. "Please, just get back in your car and allow us to do our job."

"Hell no! You will return all of that to my house. I paid for that. Morray doesn't have anything without me. That's my stuff."

I was ready to fight someone because I just was telling myself I was going to do right by her fat behind and now she wants to leave me? I hadn't complained about all the weight

she'd gained from pregnancy or anything until now. Instead of

wanting to leave, she should be grateful that I still wanted her.

Walking towards the back of the truck, I had my mind set

on unlocking the door just to see what all she thought she was

going to take. If I saw one damn statue on the back of the truck, I

was sure my hand was going to go upside Morray's head. Ten

thousand dollars a piece is what I paid for them!

"Sir, you can't do that!" The head amigo came around the

back and pushed my hand off the lock.

"Keep your damn hands off me! Do you know who I am?

I am Pastor David S. Martin!" I beat my chest and fixed my

clothes. He was going to show me the respect I commanded. I

was powerful enough to buy and sell him.

He looked around his little friends, but I could show him

better than I could tell him. All I needed was my phone which

was in the cup holder of my car. "Y'all take me to play with."

I took off to my car, but as I was walking up I saw the

Audi before I saw her. "David what are you doing? You have our neighbors looking at us crazy. As if we don't live in a White

neighborhood." Mo's voice was loud, but she wasn't yelling. She

sounded annoyed, but she was wearing these short shorts with

Denise on her arm. As mad as I was with, her I had to admire

how good she looked. Maybe the baby weight had done her well

because those hips of hers had spread, but I'd never noticed until

now.

"You think I care about them Morray? You honestly think

I care what any of these people think about us? We're richer than

everyone in this damn neighborhood." I punched the air. Most of

them were probably watching this on their security cameras.

Morray met me right by my car, looking so unbothered. Her

being so nonchalant made me want to ring her neck.

She switched Denise from one hip to another and looked

around at the workers. "I'm sorry. He will move soon. I'm sure

you all have another job to get to."

"It's ok Miss, but Juan does have somewhere else to be."

The leader of the pack spoke out. I snarled at him and turned

back to my wife, even though she wasn't acting like one.

"Senior this is done between us. I can't live like this and I know you'll never love me nor treat me the way I need to be treated. I met up with a divorce attorney." She shrugged her shoulders. Denise reached her hands out for me and I took her.

It was one thing for me to want to leave her, but for Morray to want to leave me was another thing. I made her, and it hurt honestly thinking that she didn't want me anymore; the man who made her. I showed her a million-dollar lifestyle. Then to throw in the *d-word* as if it meant nothing to her.

"Denise tell your mommy that she can't tear us apart. She doesn't want me to love you, Baby Girl." I cooed at her, hoping I was getting to her mother. I glanced up at her and reached for her hand, but she moved it. "Morray, I'm tired of this. Go inside you know we can't divorce, and besides I own you! You won't have anything without me."

There was the house, the car, the accounts, the elaborate shopping trips that she loved so much. She wasn't going to be able to afford a five-thousand-dollar weave if she left me. Morray wasn't going to leave me because I had her, and on top of all that

I would fight her for full custody of Denise.

Morray snatched Denise out of my arms, causing her to

holler. Denise was kicking and screaming, throwing her head

back having a temper tantrum and her mother just held her

against her body and laughed. I wasn't going to lose my wife like

this.

"Babe, look." I tried to reach out to her, but she shook my

hand away from her and fixed Denise on her hip. "Mo, I brought

your favorite from Godiva. Remember that vacation we were

talking about?"

I was now blocking her from leaving from by my car. She

turned to look at the inside of my car since my driver's door was

open, but she just shrugged her shoulders. There was no reason

for her to want to make this difficult. "Mo, think about it. Stay

with me and I can give you all the desires of your heart. You'll

never meet someone with as much power and money as I have."

"Senior this has nothing to do with the money. You think

I care about all of that when I'm waking up in the middle of the night only to find out that my husband isn't in our bed? I know

you're cheating on me. Now you either let me go or I can tell the

church this is just one more sin that their pastor, their leader, their

spiritual father is committing." Morray let out a soft laugh and

turned to head back to her car. She knew the conversation was

over because there was no coming back from that for me. As

much hell as I've put the church through, the last thing they

needed to know about was my marriage ending because of my

own wrong doing. As a man of God, I needed to get my life in

order.

"Are you going to move your car now?" The president of

the Mexicans wanted to speak up now that Morray had gotten in

her car.

"Man get the hell on before I have y'all deported."

Kayla Andrè

Chapter Sixteen

Geneva

"Ma'am that'll be thirty-seven dollars." The cab driver turned and faced me. Counting the bills, I had in my wallet, I contemplated giving up the only forty-dollars that I had. "Miss, it will be thirty-seven dollars. I can call the police if you don't have the money."

Not wanting to alert anyone else of my return, I decided to hand over the money and waited for my changed. The three dollars I did get back, I was going to hold on to. I prayed to God that He made Stein rot in hell for what he's done to me. When we left this country, we left with close to forty million dollars. This man left we with five grand, and being that he house was in his name, I couldn't sell it to get the money. So here I am in Tampa, hoping to fix some things and get my life back.

Getting out of the taxi, the driver came around and took my suitcases out of the trunk. Lord knows I'd never thought I would see this house once I decided to leave, but here I was

hoping that she'd forge me.

There was only a G Wagon in the driveway and I knew

she couldn't afford that on her own, but maybe she went back to

work and started trying to make money on her own. I looked

around the yard thinking to myself if I was making the right

decision of being here. I'm supposed to be dead, but here I was in

the flesh. If I had my money I wouldn't even have to be dealing

with these people, but I God had other plans for me.

I balled my hand into a fist and slammed it against the

wooden door. There wasn't any noise coming from the other side

so I decided to knock again. After about a minute, there still

wasn't any noise. Just as I was about to turn around and walk

away, thunder filled the air prompting the rain to fall.

"Liana open the door." I began to pound on the door. She

didn't have a porch so this little covering over the door wasn't

sheltering anything. "Liana!" I screamed.

Finally, I heard someone rushing to the door and the lock

being undone. As the door slowly opened, I saw her face appear.

"Oh, my god," Liana jumped back and held her chest. I knew I had frightened her, but damn it wasn't that bad. Plenty of people come back from the dead. I was sure it was in The Bible somewhere.

"Hey, can I come in? It's raining." I looked back at the rain to see it was coming down even harder.

Liana shook her head and stood right behind her door, letting me know I couldn't come in. Her eyes were still buck and she was sill staring at me, trying to see if I was really here or if I was going to disappear mid conversation like a true ghost. "What-How are you here?"

I wanted to be funny and let her know my ghost like power allowed me to teleport from Hell, but I decided to go a different route since I needed shelter from the rain. "Liana, please baby. It's raining and I don't have anywhere else to go. If you let me explain why I left,"

"No! Geneva, you can't just fake your own death and just reappear. That's not how any of this works! Do you know the problems that you've caused? They had that man in jail behind you!" Her voice rose, but she looked back behind her to see if someone was there.

"Baby, but you need to understand where my head was at. I did it for us. For you because I didn't want you to go to Hell. I was worried about your spirit and your soul. I loved you." I stepped closer to the door, making my move to get into the house. "You still love me right, Li?"

I should have known better than to show up here, but I didn't have anywhere else to go. I had my old house, but I was sure all the power and water was shut off. Besides, I didn't want to spend the money to get it cut on. If Liana didn't give in, I guess I was going to have to spend the little change I did have.

When Liana was not budging on opening the door for me, I continued to try to sweet-talk her. "Baby, please. I love you and I don't have anywhere else to go."

"Geneva, you will not get over on me again. You didn't fake your death for me, but for your own selfish reasons. You are demonic and nothing of God is within you" She opened the door wider and pointed her finger in my face.

It was either now or never, and I was damn for sure getting in that house. While her guard was down, I rushed my way into the house. I caught the little check she did earlier, like someone else was in this house and I needed to know who had replaced me. I figured it was a woman since I had turned her out.

Panic set in on her face as she tried to push me back towards the door, but I was in there now. "Liana I know someone has to be here for you to not want to let me in. I was supposed to be your wife!"

Liana placed her hands over my mouth, trying to keep my voice down, but I started kicking at her to get away. "You think I would want to marry you after how you did Pastor and your son? Get out of my house and never come back here you witch."

That was it. I had it with her name calling as if she was perfect. I cocked my fist back and slammed it into her chest. Next thing I knew, we were rolling around on the floor like a bunch of school kids. It was obvious Liana had some built-up aggression with me because she was spending blow after blow and they were landing on my face, but I was getting her too. "I hope you die for real," she shouted as she hit me.

"Liana what in the hell are you doing?" Some man's voice entered the room. The voice was so powerful that it even caused me to stop fighting, even though he only pulled Liana away. "Liana what's going on?"

"It's her!" She pointed and screamed as I lie on the floor watching the man wrapped in a towel as if he'd just gotten out of the shower. "Her! It's her."

She wasn't going to keep talking about me as if I wasn't in the room. I got up from the floor and charged at her. "Liana stop playing with me like I didn't have you screaming my name!" I reached over the man and wrapped one hand around her neck.

"Hold the hell on," the man slapped my hand down. "Who are you?" He turned around as we stood face to face and I couldn't believe who my woman had in her house.

"Troy," I questioned, already knowing that my brother was in Liana's house in nothing, but a towel.

"Babe make her go or I'm calling the police." Liana fixed her clothes, but didn't bother to come closer to me.

Did this heffa just call my bother *Babe*? Boy how a few months away can change things. Troy held his hand up to me. I guess he was trying to tell me to hold on. Then he turned his head in Liana's direction. "Bae, go in the room and wait for me, please."

Liana looked between us before she rolled her eyes at me. "Troy get this woman out of my house!"

"Liana, you trust me or not? Can you do as I say, please?" Troy turned his whole body in her direction. He was being very soft with her, not raising his voice at all. It must work with her weak behind because she surely did as she was told.

We waited until we heard the bedroom door close before we started our own conversation. "Why are you here?"

Taking the liberty to make myself home, I sat down on the sofa. "I need money. I was fine where I was, but I need money."

Troy walked over to the table in the corner where a black wallet was sitting. "Here, take this and don't come back. Your presence here will cause more bad than good." He handed me a stack of hundreds.

"But brother, I have no place to go." How could he just toss me money like I was a homeless man on the street?

"Geneva, you're dead remember? Stay dead and leave us alone."

Chapter Seventeen
David Jr.

I watched as Morray's eyes rolled to the back of her head as she reached her climax. Since she'd moved in we'd been going at it repeatedly trying to make up for lost time. Each time we finished it was as if our souls became more and more connected. The pain of her being my father's wife and her daughter being my sister was swept to the back of my thoughts.

"My gosh David," she bit her bottom lip as I went in deeper trying to finish off with her. I knew she was finished when a faint smile came across her face, and although she didn't even notice that it was there, I noticed.

Once I was done, I rolled off her and collapsed onto my side of the bed. Even though I was hot, I knew she was going to want to cuddle and I was anticipating it, but when she rolled over, I knew something was wrong.

"Morray?" I reached over and tried to pull her next to me, but she didn't budge. She shrugged her shoulder, and shook her head. "What's wrong?" I leaned over her and I saw the dampness on her face.

Before I could finish trying to see what had my girl in tears, Denise came through on the monitor, screaming. Morray sat up, but I grabbed her hand and assured her that I could handle Denise. Morray stared at me for a few seconds before she just turned over in the bed.

With Denise living with me fulltime, I was able to get more acquainted with her. She was a needy baby, but independent at the same time. Denise loved attention. She was the child to throw a temper tantrum and watch you to make sure you are watching her.

Opening the door to her room, I spotted her standing up in the crib. Her screaming was heard coming down the hallway, but as soon as I opened the door she stopped to look at me. I flicked on the lights and watched her as she crawled to the side of the crib I was closer to. She held up an empty bottle for me to take. This child was too smart for me. She let you know when she was hungry and ready to eat. Looking at the time on her cable box, I realized that it had been about four hours since she ate and she

was ready to eat again. I hated when she fell asleep early because

she would not sleep through the night.

"You are going to start making your own bottles little

girl." I reached down in her crib to pick up her and the bottle. I

almost dropped her when I heard her mother's voice. I didn't

even know she was in the room.

"I'll breastfeed her, but can you go take that milk out of

the freezer for me?" She tied the straps around her black silk robe

together before getting Denise out of my hands. "Hey Mamas.

You're up late!"

Seeing Morray with Denise made me envious that Denise

wasn't mine. I tried not to think about it, but knowing that my

father was her father sickened me and it made me want to hate

Morray, but I couldn't. She was the love of my life, which meant

I loved her daughter too. Hell, I was posting Denise all over my

snap as if she was mine.

"So, are you going to tell me why you were crying?" I

walked back in the room with a beer in my hand. Morray was

sitting up against the headboard with her legs crossed as she fed

Denise, whose eyes followed me as I made my way to the bed.

It took Morray a few seconds before she spoke, but I

knew she had a lot on her mind so I wasn't going to rush her. "I

feel like I'm just doing so wrong. I met you., fell in love, got

blackmailed into marrying your father, had his baby, and now

I'm in your house, in your bed, breastfeeding your sister. That

doesn't seem right."

Although she wasn't crying right now, I knew it had been

pulling at her because it was bothering me. "Babe, no matter

what, I love you. I know our situation isn't ideal, but that doesn't

matter. I love you more than life itself, and I'll do anything for

you and Denise. That stuff with my father, well David because he

isn't my father, we can just leave it in the past. As long as we

have each other we will be ok."

I leaned over to kiss her, to reassure her that we had each

other and that was all I needed. Something inside of me told me

to not give my all to her though. I couldn't put my finger on it.,

but something wasn't right. After she kissed me, she looked

down at Denise and I wasn't sure if that was a good thing on my end. It wasn't just a look to make sure she was still feeding, but a look of *no matter what I got you*, and I didn't know if she had me too.

After going to bed at three in the morning, I had to be back up by seven for a meeting with my coaches. Although I had been cleared, I wasn't working out as much as I should, nor was I able to practice with the team. School started in less than a month, everyone else was practicing on the field and I was just sitting there.

Football was something I knew I was destined to be great in. I knew I was going to make it to the pros and make a career out of making touchdowns, but with the tryout for the Dodgers being in a couple of days, I didn't know which dream I wanted to achieve more.

Just as I was getting in my car, my phone started to ring. The number was unsaved, but I answered it anyway. "Hello?" I pulled off onto the street and headed back to the house. Denise was supposed to be going with her father for the day so I promised my girl that I would bring her out today to show her how serious I am about making this family thing work. I may be almost nineteen, but I was smart enough not to let a good woman go.

"Is this a Mr. David S. Martin Jr.?" A woman's voice spoke up. I pulled the phone away to look at the number to see if I could recognize it in some form, but I couldn't.

"Yea, this is he. May I ask who is calling?" I transferred the call to my car Bluetooth and threw the phone down into the cup holder.

"Hello Mr. Martin, this is Jennifer Langly from the St. Joseph's Hospital. I was calling because we needed your signature in order to complete the adoption."

I took the phone away from my ear to look at it again to make sure that I wasn't trippin'. "Excuse me? Adoption? What do you mean?" I started to drive faster because of my nerves. Another call started to come through. Looking at the screen once again, I saw it was Morray. "Ma'am, give me one second."

"Sure, take your time." I switched over to Morray's line to talk to her.

"Babe?" I was trying to calm down, but trying to put together everything going on, it was hard.

"Yea, is everything ok?"

"No, just meet me at St. Joseph's. I think Hannah just pulled something slick. Just Uber there, and I'll meet you." I clicked back over to the other line before she could respond.

Trying to get all the details out of the woman, I informed her I was coming in. Even though I didn't want to be with Hannah, I didn't know how I felt about just giving up my baby. Something about that didn't seem right to me.

Once I got into the hospital, I took the elevator up to the third floor and found Ms. Langly's office. It didn't surprise me that she was a white lady with glasses that were connected to one of those beaded necklaces that the older women wear. Her nose was buried into her computer when I walked into her office, so I knocked on the door to make my presence known.

"Oh, my gosh, you scared me." She held onto her chest, but I just took a seat. I was ready to get down to business. "Are you Mr. Martin?"

"Yes, I am." I took out my phone to shoot Morray a quick text to let me know where to come to when she arrived. "So is this about the baby I share with Hannah?"

She searched her cluttered desk for something. "Yes, but just give me one second while I find the folder." I was annoyed with the fact that she called me and didn't have anything together. "Ms. Donaldson has signed over her legal rights as the mother of this precious little boy, but since she did list you as the father, we have to, by law, acknowledge this. There is a couple willing, and ready, to take care of him, but if you choose not to sign over your rights, it's saying that you want to keep him and raise him yourself."

I took in her words and just nodded my head so that she knew I was listening to her. She first lost me when she said that it was a precious little boy. On top of that, how was there a family already waiting. Hannah hadn't told me anything about adoption.

The way she was talking about raising the child, I never would've thought that idea crossed her mind.

"Mr. Martin, did you hear me?" I snapped out of my trance and looked back at her. "I know this may be a hard decision, but I do have to inform you that you have eight months to renege on your word."

"This is a lot to take in. I don't know what I want to do, honestly." I ran my hands along my hands as I tried to stop my palms from clamming up. "When was the baby born?"

She looked over the file, using her pointer finger. "Two nights ago. Ms. Donaldson signed over her rights this morning. If you want to see him," she paused mid-sentence because of a knock at the door. Of course, it was Morray.

"Hi, I'm here with him." She pointed at me as the woman welcomed her to have a seat. She kissed my lips and then waited for the conversation to continue.

"As I was saying, if you want to meet him you can. He's in the nursery and I can show you down there." She rested her elbows on her desk and waited.

Morray looked over at me really confused. "Hannah had the baby, a boy. She signed over her parental rights and now it's time for me to decide if I want to do the same." I reached out and took her hand into mine.

"Is this your wife?" The lady pried into my business, but Morray proudly answered her, with a lie. "Such a beautiful ring you have." Now even that caught my attention. Looking down at Morray's hand I saw the wedding set that my father had given her resting perfectly on her ring finger. I brought my eyes back up to meet hers and tilted my head to the side to let her know how confused I was.

Morray slowly pulled her hand away from mine. "Thank you," was all she said while trying to look away from me, but I was damn for sure going to address this later.

The lady asked me once more if I wanted to see the boy, and I gave in. I still was torn between being there for him and letting him go. How would he think of me when he got older knowing that his parents didn't fight to keep him? On the way up to the nursery, Morray walked right by my side. She reached her hand out to catch mine, but I knocked it off. She brought herself up to the hospital to meet me with the ring that my father gave her. That was the biggest slap to my face.

I knew she was going to have an excuse, but I was sure it wasn't going to be good enough. No matter what we went through, she always did something to mess us up. I hated myself for loving her so much. Most of the women I slept with didn't get anything close to the amount of attention that I gave to Morray. She was my everything, and I felt like I didn't measure up to much in her eyes.

"So what are you thinking?" Morray stood in front of me as I held my son. Damn that sounds crazy just thinking about the fact that I had a son. "He's handsome."

"I don't know Morray. I'm not in a place now where I can take care of a child. I mean you did just move in with Denise, but still it's different." My eyes stayed locked on him. This little boy was so innocent. The more I held him, the more I didn't want to bring him into my family.

My family had a way of ruining people and Morray was a perfect example. When I had just met her she had a beautiful and light spirit, but as of now she was a perfect Martin. No regards to anyone, but herself. I could say that she did care about Denise, which is more than what I could say about everyone else in my family. Hell, my grandmother didn't even come around like a typical grandmother. There were no home videos of everyone sitting around the living room opening gifts on Christmas morning. I opened my gifts alone while my father sat in his study, drinking, and my mother sat in her bathroom getting done up by stylists so that she would look nice when we attended church later that day.

There was no way I wanted that for him. "Do you know the family he's going with?"

"Yes, but they are asking for a closed adoption so I am not at liberty to say anything. The only thing I can say or do is that you will be listed on the birth certificate as his father. That way if he does choose to reach out, he'll know who he is looking for." She stood by the door and just let me have my moment.

I wasn't a punk, but this made me shed a tear. A son, my son, and I had to give him up. "I love you, Man. I'll never forget you. Come and find me, please." I kissed his forehead and handed him back to the nurse.

There was no way for me to control my cries. They wouldn't stop. This was the hardest thing I had to do in my life. Give up my son for him to have a better life than I had. I stood in the hallway and held on to Morray. I needed her, and I hated that I needed her. She was my rock, and she was held me up in the middle of the hallway.

"You did the best thing for him, Baby. You did what you felt would be best. You did it because you love him. Rather you know it yet or not." As she consoled me, my cries started to ease up. "He won't be mad at you."

Her last words made me look up at her. "How do you know that? How would you feel knowing that your parents couldn't do right by you? How would that make you feel huh Morray? You're walking around here like your behind doesn't stink when you use the bathroom, but it does. You think you can run back and forth between he and I, but that will stop. You should've given Denise up for adoption instead of subjecting her to these crazy people she has to call family. I guess you didn't do it because you don't love her like you say you do, but you don't know it yet, huh?"

Morray's eyes grew wider with each word that fell off of my lips. Once I was finished and had realized what I said, it was too late to take it back. "Baby, I'm sorry. I didn't mean that." I reached my arms out to get her, but she raised her hand.

"No David. I get it." She bit her bottom lip, and then turned away to leave.

When I looked around, the people surrounding us were watching. "What are y'all looking at? I'm sure y'all have seen more explicit stuff on reality television."

"You want to sign those papers now?" The little lady appeared out of thin air with her pointer finger in the air.

"Yea, let me do that." Now I'd lost a son, and I knew I had lost Morray once again.

Eighteen

Kayla Andrè

Pastor David

"So you're saying that the tumor is bigger?" My spirit was slowly exiting my body and I couldn't catch it. How could a tumor double in size in a matter of weeks? "Is there something we can do?"

My doctor looked back over the charts before he closed them and stood up from the stool. "Mr. Martin, we can do a surgery. That way we can test it and see if it is cancerous or not. I'm just going off of my expertise by saying it is, but I do want to let you know that a tumor of this magnitude can kill you if we don't go forward with a surgery."

I guess this was God's way of getting me back for all the wrong I had done in my life. "About how long?" My thumbs were at war in my lap, but it felt as though the world was at a standstill.

"A tumor that size, usually about six weeks without surgery." He placed his hand on my shoulder as if he was trying to comfort me, but how can you comfort somebody after telling them they were going to die in less than six months.

Dr. Myer asked me several times if I wanted to schedule a surgery, but something about the surgery scared me. Everyone that I knew who had cancer, died in surgery. That made me wonder if the surgery would kill me sooner than the cancer would. I would have to pray on that particular decision. Don't really know why I was praying anyways, this was God's doing.

Once I got home I was quickly reminded me how much I'd lost. The house was so quiet and there wasn't a fruity aroma that hit your nose when you entered the front door. Everything was so cold, literally. The temperature in the house stayed on sixty degrees. The icy feeling felt like my heart was living on the outside.

"WHY GOD?" I punched the wall in my foyer. "WHY DID YOU HAVE TO DO THIS?"

I knew I had done things that weren't in His will, but that was just my flesh speaking. I knew what was right. How were there atheist out here living better than anyone else, but Christians lived hard lives? That didn't seem fair to me. Even as a grown man I wanted things to be done fairly. He could've killed all of them off, but no He makes His own people sick so that we could have a testimony.

It didn't take long for me to finish the entire bottle of Hennessy. By the time I took my last sip, I found myself laying in the tub, fully clothed. On my way home, I'd stopped by one of the church member's homes who I knew sold marijuana, and got enough to roll two blunts.   I was so zoned out, that I heard Morray's voice, and I felt like God had already called me home. "Morray, where are you?" I held my hands out for her to bring me to The Lord. "Morray?" I kept searching, but everything was black.

"Open your damn eyes, you big dummy!" The stiffness of her hand coming across my face scared me. "Why did you call me, and why in the hell does it smell like weed in here?"

Seeing her in front of me, in the flesh, made me ecstatic. Well maybe that and the fact that I wasn't actually dead. "Baby, you're here. You love me." I rushed the get out of the jacuzzi tub, but fell flat on my face.

My vision was blurry, but I knew where everything was from memory. I was so drunk that my legs weren't working. I had to crawl towards her in order to stand up, but every inch I moved closer to her, Morray moved further back. I had to follow her into the bedroom.

I felt as if she was teasing me, but I wanted her so badly. Just a piece or her, or at least that was what I was telling myself. Getting Morray into the bed, with no clothes on, so I could remind her why she married me. "Baby, come give Daddy some of that sugar." My back was against the bed as I rested on the floor. Morray was standing in front of me with her arms folded. Intoxicated or not, I still knew the definition of her body. My vision may not have been 20/20, but the way her hips stood out further from waist was making me stand at attention down there.

"Senior, what in the hell is wrong with you. I'm not going there with you. Why did you blow up my phone?" She knocked my hand away as I was reaching for her. "Stop trying to touch me. Go touch that old hag you were sleeping with."

Miranda had slipped my mind. After Morray left me and revealed she knew I was cheating, I stopped talking to Miranda. She didn't have anything on me, so there was no reason as to why I needed to deal with her. She was the reason as to why my marriage failed.

"I'm dying Mo. Baby I'm dying." I cried out for her, but she still just stood there and watched me. "You don't hear me Mo?"

I didn't know what was going through her mind because she wasn't saying anything and my vision was not clear enough to see her facial expression, but I could guess that she was chewing on the inside of her jaw, thinking.

I was ready to beg to get my family back, but the words were coming to my lips slower than the excess alcohol that caused me to spill my guts all over the floor.

"Are you eff'ing kidding me Senior! You are too grown to be throwing up like a rookie." Her screaming was tuned out by my own gagging as my body tried to rid itself of the toxins.

God must've heard some prayer I'd said this time because me throwing up made Morray stay with me. Matter of fact, she and Denise stayed with me. Well they didn't stay in my room, but they did stay in the house. Waking up the next morning, my head felt like it had a million little needles stabbing it.

Morray woke me up with a glass of some concoctions. "What is this?" I took it from her, but I had to examine it before I put it in my mouth. It was red and thick.

"It's an old family recipe to cure hangovers, but drink it. We need to talk." Because I was a man, I took the disgusting drink like a champion. The stiff drink tasted like a mixture of tomato juice and ginger. The worst drink in the world, but I did start to feel better in a few minutes.

Denise sat down on the bed with me while her mom went to go bring the glass down to the kitchen and take a phone call. She didn't say anything, but I knew it was DJ. Hell, the fact that her ringtone was *Dangerously In Love* by Beyoncé didn't hurt my chances of being correct.

Kayla Andrè

The baby that we'd taken home with us was not so small anymore. Almost one and sitting like she was about to make twenty-one. Even with the two pig-tails and butterfly onesie, she still sat with her legs crossed, back against the pillows, with holding her bottle.

"Baby girl," she looked at me through the corners of her eyes. I don't know what it was, but she didn't seem as happy to be around me like she used to. "Denise, don't be like that." I reached out to grab her, but she threw her bottle to the ground and laid out having a hissy fit.

Of course, that sent Morray running into the room asking me what happened as if I didn't know how to take care of my own flesh a blood. "Don't do that Morray. I am her farther."

She snatched Denise into her arms so fast, rocking her from side to side. "Yes, but knowing you, you tried to pull her to you. Remember the other day she had a problem when I left her with you."

"Bet she doesn't act like that with DJ," I mumbled under my breath. Morray had to hear me, but she didn't respond to my remark. I laid back down as she went to go rinse of the bottle just

to give it back to Denise.

When she got back in the room, she sat down on the bed,

keeping Denise in her arms. "We need to talk. So about you

dying?" Damn, I almost thought Geneva was sitting in front of

me because she sounded so harsh with her words.

"The doctor told me if I don't have surgery, I could be

looking at only about six weeks. I don't want to think about this."

I flicked my wrist in the air and pulled the sheets over my body.

Looking down, I finally realized I was naked. "Did we?"

Morray let out the loudest laugh that made Denise look at

her. "Senior, no!" That must've just tickled her little spirit

because she started slapping her thigh.

She hurt my pride with that one. Made me feel as though

I'm a joke or something. I wanted to come back with something

slick, but I knew that would put me off in a worse situation than I

am in now. I wanted to plead to Morray, asking her not to let me

die alone. I knew I didn't deserve her love, but nobody deserves

to die alone, right?

"Mo, baby please come home. With only six weeks, I just want you and my daughter. I want to right all my wrongs. Don't make me go through this alone. God has shown me how wrong I've done you and everyone else that loved me, but please Baby. I love you, and I'm willing to spend my last days showing you how sorry I am."

Morray sat there with another blank stare, a poker face. "You think that because you are dying that I'm supposed to just forget everything that you've done to me? No! Life doesn't work like that! Nothing works like that!" Oh how quickly that laughing came to a halt.

I was serious about proving to her how much I loved her. She needed to believe me, but I knew she wasn't. "Can we do it for Denise, please? Allow me to spend these last days with my child. Even if we don't do it as husband and wife, let me have this time with this."

The look on her face let me know she was thinking about it. I looked down at Denise who was holding out her empty bottle for me to take. She didn't want me to touch her, but she wanted to give me her dirty dishes. Yea, I took it from my child, but I wanted to be stubborn and show her how she hurt my feelings.

"Why not go through with the surgery Senior? I thought they didn't even know if it was cancerous." She kept her eyes fixed on me, waiting for me to answer her question.

"Everyone I knew with cancer that decided to have surgery either died in surgery or died as a result of the surgery. I'm not doing that. It's death sentence either way so I'd rather die happy, with my family by my side." I threw in the last part hoping that she would give in and say *yes* to me moving back home.

With such a heavy conversation taking place, the room was quiet, but Denise didn't care. She crawled from her mother's lap over to me with a huge smile over her face. Before I knew it, there was a smile on my face. Drool was hanging from her lip as she gave me a wet kiss on my nose. "Da!" She clapped her hands and looked back at her mother, and then back over to me.

"Da!" She pointed at me and then cheered. I grabbed her to tackle her with hugs and kisses. Yes, I know you're thinking about the fact that I was naked, playing with my child. There were covers between us and she couldn't see anything, but my chest.

This was what I wanted. I wanted to have this bonding time with my child before God took me out of here. The relationship between David Jr. and I was gone and I don't think there would ever be a way for us to reconnect so all I had was Denise.

Yes, I did want to bond with him, but between the lies of his mother and the fact that I married the love of his life, and had a baby, I don't think he'll forgive me. I still made sure he was taken care of though. He didn't know this, but I paid Andre's parents for the first six months of his rent. Not only did I do that, but I told Steven about the Dodgers connect. Everything he thought happened by chance, happened because I made it happen. He was still my son, blood or not, and I loved him even with all the wrong I had done.

Sometimes I wondered if he and I would still have a relationship if I would've left Morray alone, but as quickly as the thought came it left. Although it cost me DJ, my relationship with Morray was a blessing. I loved this girl, and I didn't care what anyone had to say about it. Yes, she may have been about twenty years younger than I was, but she brought out a side of me that I didn't know existed. Not only that, but she gave me my daughter. Morray gave birth to the only Martin female in two generations. The amount of power that came with Denise's birth ran a lot deeper than most could imagine, but that's not what this is about.

"Senior," Morray's soft voice caught my attention. "I'll stay only because of Denise, but please respect the fact that I want to be with David. I love you because you gave me the best thing that has ever happened to my life, but I'm no longer in love with you. I forgive you for the hurt you've caused me, but I pray that you can forgive me too."

When she was finished talking, I had no choice, but to accept her on her terms. "Thank you; for everything."

Chapter Nineteen

Liana

Everyone loves to think that I'm just a confused church member that got caught up with Geneva, but that was kind of true. Before dealing with Geneva, I had my head on straight. I did what The Bible told me to do, and when my marriage failed, I even tried to follow God's words then as well. Never did I thought I would fall in love with a woman. I can tell you one thing for sure, I wasn't born that way. It was something that just happened. Was I confused? I don't know, but I do know I loved that woman and she hurt me more than anyone else has ever.

The thing with Geneva that hurt most was the fact that she faked her death. Then for her to show up on my doorstep as if I was supposed to take her back was another thing. I may have been just a little confused, but I damn for sure wasn't a dumb bunny.

My situation with Troy was different though. After I thought Geneva was dead, I was lost. Troy saw me around church and decided to be my friend. Never did I think me using his shoulder to cry on would mean I would be bent over the arm of my sofa while he pleasured me from the back with his mouth, and that turned into nightly sessions of passionate love making.

Troy and I were meant to be, or so I thought. Ever since the day Geneva came back he and I had not spoken. Not even a simple text message. I did try to reach out once, but he didn't respond so I moved on. That was until I my period showed up late. At first I thought it was menopause, but when the doctor confirmed the positive pregnancy result, I knew I needed to talk to him.

I had searched everywhere for him, but he was nowhere to be found. The last place I could think to look was Pastor David's house, but I didn't want to go. I knew Morray and I weren't what you would call friends and for sure Pastor David wasn't trying to be civil with me after I accused him of killing his ex-wife.

Luckily for me when I rolled past the house, the gates were open so I drove right on in. Troy's car was parked right in front next to a Bentayga, but I didn't see Morray's Audi. She must've upgraded. That was the type of car I deserved to drive. Honestly, I had never seen anything like it in my life, but I knew that it cost upwards of two-hundred grand and I knew my child deserved to live like them.

Maybe Kimora wasn't brought up the best way, but I was sure to get it right with this baby. Having a baby at forty-three wasn't ideal, but I was going to rock it like those actresses in Hollywood.

I knocked on that door with vengeance. It felt like they couldn't hear me, but they had those big heavy knockers on the door so no matter how big the house was, I knew it made some noise. My time waiting let me admire the home. It was much bigger the Geneva's, but something about it still felt like you were at home.

"Liana?" Morray's voice came over the speaker.

"Yes ma'am. May I come in?" I put on my nice voice, hoping that there wouldn't be any drama.

There was a buzzing sound and then Morray appeared at the door with Denise on her hip. She eyed me up and down and just stood there like she wasn't trying to let me in, but of course I played crazy and slid in around her. People already thought I didn't have all of my marbles so why not just continue the charade.

"Liana, is there anything I can do to help you? If you are here to see the pastor, he and Troy are in a meeting. Please take off your shoes if you're going to stay. There are new flip-flops by the door for our guests, take one." She spoke with annoyance as she led the way to the living room. Even taking my shoes off I felt like they had money. They golden container held anywhere between fifty to sixty pairs of shoes. My child had to live like this. I was going to live like this. Morray continued to talk, and I was trying to listen to her, but I was so caught up in the décor of the home that I couldn't focus on anything else.

When I walked in I felt like either I was in Egypt or that I was in some African kingdom. The double staircase that had a black and gold railing spoke to me, and the big letter M that was monogrammed in gold on the floor made me feel like I didn't want to step on it. Looking up at the celling you saw the huge crystal chandelier lit up the foyer had to cost more than my car. It looked like it opened to a third story.

"Liana?" Morray called out to me. My head turned back to her direction and I was even more amazed how the living room looked that was straight ahead. Everything was gold and white. Even the sofa was trimmed in gold. Not to mention that the carpet was white. Cocaine white. No, this carpet was as white as the suites the deaconess board wore on Communion Sunday.

Morray offered me something to drink while I waited. I only took it because I wanted to see what type of glasses she used. I wasn't impressed when I got my glass of ice water in a plain simple glass. I don't know what I expected, but it sure wasn't a dog-on cylinder.

"I'm actually here waiting on Troy." I decided to inform her so she didn't think I cared about her damn husband. No matter if Geneva was alive or not, I knew for a fact David's behind was no good.

The tension in the room was thick because Morray sat across from me on the throne like chair with Denise on her lap, both of their eyes burning holes into my head. I was getting uncomfortable, but I couldn't leave because I was there for a reason. I even had two of my pregnancy tests in my purse for proof.

"Well I'm happy to see Denise doing well." I smiled at the little girl who didn't bother to return the gesture.

"Thank you. It's a blessing she is still here. God allowed my baby to survive all that she's been through." Morray turned Denise around to face her, tickling her, and showering her with kisses. The little girl giggled loudly and tried to tickle her mother back. Seeing their bond made me feel guilty. Almost like everything was coming back to memory that I had tried to block.

My hand unconsciously made its way to my stomach as I watched the both of them in envy. I prayed that this time God gave me a boy because I don't think I did such a great job with a girl. It could've been because I tried to teach her how to be a woman when I didn't know how to be a woman myself.

"Did they ever say if it was the arsenic that almost killed or was it anything else?" The question was spoken before I had a chance to process the consequences that would come from it. From the way Morray's eyes squinted as she locked in on me, even sitting Denise on the floor, I knew I had just given myself away.

"How did you know about the arsenic? Senior nor myself told anyone about it." She rose from her seat and made her way over me to me. "Liana, how do you know?"

My tongue had become heavy because I wasn't able to speak. I felt as though I was mute and God had taken my voice from me. He must've taken my reflexes too because I wasn't even able to block the punch that Morray sent to the right side of my face. The metal taste that came to my taste buds alerted me that she had drew blood.

Morray wasn't trying to stop herself because she grabbed me by my shirt and flung me to the ground. "How do you know. Answer me now."

Once I was on the ground I knew I could kick her, but even that didn't help. She must've had some sort of super strength because she taking my kicks like a man as well as delivering punches that made me want to scream bloody murder.

"How do you know Liana? Did you poison my child you sadistic bastard?" With each word, there was a blow to my face. I was in too much pain to fight back, but I knew I had to protect my stomach. If there was any chance of me having a better life, I needed to protect my stomach at all costs.

I don't know what sent them running in, but I was glad when I heard the voices of David and Troy. They pulled us apart, but Morray still had her hand wrapped around my hair. She was reaching over Troy to continue to beat me.

"Morray stop it. Denise is practically screaming because of your actions and you don't even know it." David grabbed her then tossed her on the sofa. "What in the hell is going on anyways?"

Troy was standing in front of me, blocking me from anymore abuse, but his head was turned towards Morray. "Troy,"

I spoke his name, but as soon as I opened my mouth the blood

began to pour out of it.

"Sit here, I'll get you something." He sat me down on the

floor and rushed out of the room. Morray tried to cease the

opportunity, but David grabbed her by her arm.

"No, forget all of this. This big raggedy Satanist whore

poisoned my daughter. She was the one to put the arsenic in her

formula! That Juwanna man looking whore right there David." I

looked around to see if Troy had heard the accusations and

spotted him coming in from the kitchen. His eyes were narrowed

in on me.

My heart stopped. I knew I shouldn't have brought my

behind over here. I was doing good too. Keeping this secret for

months with no one suspecting anything, but I just got so nervous

sitting in front of Morray.

"Did you do it?" Troy handed me the napkin. Before I

could reply I wanted to take a second and look at him. If I told

the truth, I risked losing everything I wanted, but if I lied I knew

God would punish me some type of way.

I lowered my eyes down to the cuffs of his button-down shirt that has a little blood on both of them because of me. In that moment, I thought of my whole life and the choices I made that had brought me to this very moment. Stupid wasn't even the word to describe how I felt. Ever since I got involved with Geneva, my life took a turn for the worse.

"Say something diabolical wench." Morray yelled from across the room. She standing up with David holding her by her waist so that she couldn't get to me. I can't say I didn't deserve her licks, but I am happy they broke it up.

Denise was sitting on the floor still and seeing her brought tears to my eyes. Knowing that I was the one who could've taken her away from this Earth all because I thought that her farther killed my lover made me want to kill myself.

"I didn't mean to. I just was hurt, and I didn't think. Troy, you have to forgive me. When she didn't respond to me texting her phone I didn't know what to do. I stopped texting her if that helps." I reached my hands out to him, but he pulled back, shaking his head. He brought his hand up to his mouth like he was thinking about something. My chances with him were probably over because of that, but I still needed to let him know about our baby. "Troy, please. I'm pregnant."

"You're the one stalking me about my husband too? Nah, come take this beat down like a woman since you're so bold behind a phone and sick enough to want to kill a baby!" Morray screamed from the sofa, but I rolled my eyes at her. Now was not the time for foolishness.

The spotlight had fallen on me. I stood up to prepare myself for my speech. This had to be something good because I'd already lost him. From the looks of it, my speech probably wouldn't help. They say nothing beats failure, but a try.

"Look, Troy, just hear me out. I know what I did was wrong. Hell, it was evil, but my mindset back then was not what it is now. God has forgiven me so I'm asking you to as well. Do this for our child. Before you say it's not yours remember that you are the first man I've slept with since my ex-husband and there is no possible way that Geneva could've gotten me pregnant. Remember the things we talked about late at night when we had pillow talk. I'm still that same girl, but I made a few mistakes. I can't lose you. We can't lose you." I placed my hand on my stomach to add volume to my statements.

My face was wet, and my jaw was hurting. I just needed to get Troy to understand that I was sincere. I know I would never do what I did to Denise again. I don't even know what possessed me to do that in the first place. It had to be a demon. The part about me stalking Morray was funny. I just wanted her to understand that her life wasn't so perfect.

Troy didn't say a word, but he kept his eyes on me as if he was studying me. My throat felt like there was a lump stuck in it and I couldn't get it to go all the way down. My palms were clamming up and the pit of arms felt as though I was fresh out the shower with no towel to dry with.

"See you keep apologizing to me, but it was not my daughter who you tried to kill," I had to stop him because he was getting it wrong.

"No, I was just trying to make her sick." I help my hand up in defense.

"Senior, I'ma beat her again. Better get that *Jack and the Bean Stalk* built skank out of my house." Morray was shaking in her seat. I felt like my life was in danger and I needed to get out of here. I walked over to the sofa to get my purse in order to leave. "I'm calling the police. I'm sending her behind to prison."

Now what happened next surprised the spirit in my body. David hit Morray's hand so hard that her phone fell to the floor. Troy rushed over to her and the both stood over her like beasts. "Mo don't ever in your life involve the police in my business. Not unless I call them myself."

I felt as though they were on my side again. If the police weren't going to be called, nothing else could happen that could scare me. With that being said, I grabbed my purse and thought I was sneaking away, but Troy called my name. Damn, I guess I have to be quicker than that.

"Yea?" I turned around, trying to put on a sad face, but in the back of my mind I was happy that he acknowledged me.

"I'll pass by your house later tonight, but you need to apologize before you go if you want us to work." He nodded his head towards Morray. Baby if all I needed to do was say sorry to the wide trick he should've been said that.

I gave an Oscar worthy performance, even bringing the tears back. "Morray I promise you, I don't even sleep at night knowing the damage I have done to you and your daughter. I know that I deserve to die for that I did, but I am asking that you forgive me. Know that it was not me that did this to you, but a demon that attacked my spirit and because my faith wasn't where it should have been, that demon won. I shall spend the rest of my days asking you to forgive me.

As for me texting and calling you, I'm sorry about that too. God really isn't done with me and every day I am striving to become a better woman and a better Christian."

Once I was finished, I wiped my face and looked down at the floor. I even impressed myself with everything I said. Maybe I should've been an actress instead of a nurse. Morray didn't think I did good though. When she didn't say anything, I lifted my head.

Kayla Andrè

She was still sitting in between Troy and David. Her arms were folded and her face was red and wet. Even with her skin being brown you could clearly see the red undertones and she was shaking, and her eyes seemed to be made of glass.

"Get. Out. Of. My House." She spoke the words through her clenched tight teeth. She didn't have to tell me twice. Troy had already said he would come by my house later and that's all I needed him to do. I knew once I laid this thing back on him, he'd be back under my spell.

Chapter Twenty

First Lady Morray

To say I was done with Senior was an understatement. Not allowing me to call the police, and for him and Troy to stand over me like I was the one who poisoned my child was too much for me to handle. DJ and I weren't on the best of terms and it wasn't fair of me to always run to him when I had problems in my marriage. Although he and I did speak about the fact that I was only home because his father was dying, I don't think he truly understood. For those reason, I locked Denise and I in the guest suite for the entire night. I didn't eat and when she wanted to eat, I breastfed her because I refused to face him.

Who would've thought that out everyone who could've poisoned my child it would be Liana, and even though the texts and phone calls had stopped, it felt good knowing they would never come again. Now I didn't care for her, personally, but I didn't think she and I were so at odds where she would want to kill my child. Even if she was doing it to get back at Senior, it wasn't just Senior's daughter she was doing it to. Yea, I know

The Bible says that we should forgive, but I didn't know if I was

that much of a Christian for me to forgive Liana.

I had been in my room since two o'clock the day before

and with the clock saying that it was just a little past noon, I

knew I needed to eat. So, after taking a shower, getting Denise

and myself dressed for the day, and then feeding her I decided

that it was safe to go get my own self something to eat. By the

time, I was ready to leave out of the room, Denise had fallen

asleep. So, I decided that I'd let her stay upstairs in bed while I

went down to the kitchen. Of course, I had the video baby

monitor with me so I could keep an eye on her.

The kitchen was on the other side of the house meaning

there was a good chance I would run into Senior. I listened

closely to see if I could hear any movements or anything, but I

didn't so I figured the coast was clear. That wouldn't last long

because not even two bites into my scrambled egg sandwich, he

came in all bare chest with a pair of joggers. To say this man was

sick, there was no indication from his physique. He was still as muscular as the day I'd met him, maybe a little bit more now that

he'd been in jail. I was still very much physically attracted to my

husband and somewhat in love. He gave me my first child so

don't sit up there and judge me.

Senior came sat at the table next to me, taking the video

monitor and staring at it. "You'll never know how much I love

you because of what you gave me. This baby is the most precious

thing I've ever had."

How dare he say that after he let that woman go after she

revealed what she'd done to my child, his child! I threw my

sandwich down on the plate and stood up from the table. He'd

just made me lose my appetite. I wasn't hungry anymore. If I

didn't have God in my heart, I'd let the sick bastard die alone.

"Morray, stop!" He blocked me from leaving the kitchen.

We were chest to chest. Well not exactly because he was taller

than me, but still with the anger I had built up, I was sure I could

take him today. "You don't think I just let her go free do you?"

I looked out him as if he had *Boo Boo the Fool* written

across his forehead because that's just how stupid he looked asking me that after I saw the woman walk away. "Yes Senior.

Yes I do think you let her get away. She walked her bad built

behind up out of my house untouched besides the blood that I

drew, and I bet not catch her again. She's going to wish you let

me call the police because every time I see her I'm going to beat

her! Again, and again!"

A smirk came across his face as if he thought I was

playing with him. I had about enough of him and his games, so I

squared up for a fight. "You know I love when you're angry. It's

just so sexy." He sat the monitor down on the counter and started

walking me into the island behind me.

Him being this close to me was making me a little

nervous. Not like I was scared of him, but nervous as in I was a

high school girl and he was my crush. I still pushed him so he

knew that I meant business, but that didn't stop him from

wrapping his arms around me and lifting me onto the island so

that he could stand in between my legs. No, he was not about to

get it that easy.

"Stop fighting me Mo and just listen." He still had one

arm wrapped around me as he blocked my punches with the

other, all while trying to kiss on my neck. Yea, he was for sure

turning me on, but in the back of my mind I knew this was

disrespectful to my relationship with David.

"Senior, no! We aren't going there. You had me, but you

lost me. You lost me and you let that wildebeest try to kill my

child. I hate you." I tried pushing him away, but he wrapped both

arms around me and started sucking on my ear.

My ear was my weak spot and he knew it. No matter how

much I tried to deny the warmth sensation that was brewing

between my legs. Although David was a pro in the bed room, it

was like Senior invented sex. Still, I needed to know about Liana.

Nothing was going to block me finding out about what's going to

happen to her. In my eyes, she needed the death penalty.

"St-stop! No! What's going to happen to Liana?" I moved

my head away from him so that I could look him in his eyes.

Senior stood up straight before he started to talk.

"Morray, I'm far from being the average man. My power runs

deep. My family has ties to everything from recreational drugs to placing a man in The White House. Trust me," he paused to move the seams of my Nike shorts to the side to slide a finger inside of me. My back arched, but I was still trying to listen to what he was saying. "Mark my words when I say Liana may have thought when she left here last night that everything was good, but I promise you she didn't go to sleep thinking that."

"What? What does that mean Senior? You always talk in damn riddles. Tell me!" I raised my voice so he could clearly hear me. "Answer me!" He stuck another finger inside of me, twirling them around. I'm pretty sure my eyes rolled to the back of my head.

He moved his hand behind my neck and started working his fingers. "Don't worry about it. Just know she's sorry." My mouth was open, but I kept my eyes locked in his as I watched the expression on his face as he brought my body pleasure. "You missed me, huh? You want to see how much I missed you?"

You're damn skippy I want to see how much you missed me, but I couldn't get my mouth to form those words so I just nodded my head. Senior took his fingers out of me and scooped

me up, bringing me up to our bedroom, but not before I grabbed

the baby monitor. I took a glance at it just to make sure Denise

was still sleeping.

The way this man threw me on the bed and snatched off

my clothes as if he'd been preparing for this moment for months

made me climax right there before he even touched me again. I

watched as he took of his pants and boxers trying to anticipate his

next move. He came to the edge of the bed and grabbed my

thighs so that my behind was barely on the bed before he got

down on his knees and placed his head down there.

I lost count how many times I released myself. Especially

when he told me to hold on to the footboard of the bed and lifted

me into the air, only to slide inside of me from the back. The

positions and the things we did then were way more out of the

box than the things we did when we were together. The thing I

was most excited about was that he didn't even seem to want me

to go down on him. His words to me were that this was all about me, and that he was showing me how sorry he was for

everything.

Tears started to rush from their ducts as we finished in a

missionary position and he recited the same vows that he told me

on our wedding day. "For richer or wealthier because as long as I

have you, I could never be poor. In sickness or in health. No

matter what the doctor's say, I know with you I can never be

sick. You are my medicine and you'll always make me well

again. Not even death could do us part, and I'll never leave your

side. There isn't anything that I can't accomplish when I have

you by my side. You've made me into a new person; a better

person. My cup runneth over with love for you. Everything I do

now, and forever will be for you."

With each stroke, he recited another line from what he'd

told me months before. I didn't know If I was crying because of

how much he was telling me he loved me or how much I knew he

was lying. I believed every word he spoke to me on our wedding

day, and even the one when he said he promised me a lifetime of

fidelity.

"You love me baby?" He lifted his head to look at my face. "Why are you crying Mo? Don't cry please. I'm sorry, Baby. Just stop, please?" He rolled off me and laid next to me, bringing me into his chest.

That made me cry harder. I didn't even know why I was crying so hard. My mind couldn't pin-point a reason, but I know that I just couldn't stop. The more he tried to get me to stop the harder I cried. It was like every emotion I'd been holding spilled out. It could've been my failed marriage or even that I was married in the first place. I didn't know if it was because of finding out about what all Liana has done or betraying David by sleeping with his father again, but whatever it was, it was coming out.

"Can you tell me why you're crying?" Senior kissed my forehead. I brought my eyes to look up at him and shrugged my shoulders. I didn't know this man.

Yea I was married to him, had a child for him, and even allowed him inside of me raw, but I didn't know who he was. I knew his son, his ex-wife, best friend, and very few family members, but I didn't know anything about him. Who was he? Where did he come from, and why did he act the way he did? I was so blinded about the blackmail and then the material things he threw my way that I didn't even focus on who he could be.

"Who are you? I found a box in your hidden room some time back and there were letters and keys, but nothing that allowed me to put the pieces together. How does your family have their hands in so much that they can put someone in The White House? Did you kill Geneva? Did you purposefully try to create a baby with me? Why would you take me from your son?"

I sat up in the bed and waited for him to answer. It took him some time too. It was like he wasn't sure if he wanted to tell me. "Tell me the truth Senior or this," I moved my pointer finger back between the both of us, "This is done."

"Do I have your loyalty?" He fixed himself against the headboard and waited for his answer.

"Yes Senior. You see I didn't call the police when you asked me not to. I'm here with you when you saw you're dying, but to say you have a tumor on your lung you sure don't have sex like you do." I pulled the flat sheet over my breasts because the

air had just kicked in.

He licked his lips before he said anything. "My family

isn't your average family. Hell, I don't know how to describe it.

We're very powerful, but we got here by doing a lot of

underhanded things. My great-great-grandfather was born into

slavery and he refused to die that way. He became the pastor of

his plantation. He was the only slave that his master owned who

could read and write. He married his wife and she bore him all

sons, but only one daughter who was said to be the apple of his

eye.

One day when the girl turned about eleven she started to

become a woman, and the master took an interest into her. Now

as slaves, there isn't too much her parents could do to stop it from

happening. Needless to say, the girl got pregnant. Because she

was so young, her body couldn't handle childbirth so she died

giving birth to a son. It angered my grandfather so that he and his

other sons planned to kill the entire plantation, and they did.

Setting everything on fire, even the slave quarters. There was only one other family saved and that was so my family could still procreate.

I don't know all of the details, but the other family was of some relation of Geneva which was why our marriage was arranged. They lived in the woods like savages, killing everyone that came as a threat or anyone they considered to be a threat. So many people started coming up missing that a man by the name of George T. Martin, a White man, became suspicious and went searching for an answer. Before you ask, yes, we got our last name from a White man. Anyways, somehow he discovered my family out there, but when he was captured he spoke with my grandfather about a way to make my family free in the real world. All they had to do was pretty much threaten everyone into electing him the town's mayor. We took our last name from him, and became professional murderers.

The other family wasn't into it as much was mine were so they escaped up North, but somehow the two families managed to stay in contact. My family was only free in whatever area that Mr. Martin presided over so they got him as far up as congress.

By the time slavery was abolished my family had our hand in so many different things that we had so much money we didn't know what to do with it.

Even with all of that, my grandfather never stopped teaching the word of God. Our church had been in our family for generations. Even as professional murders, we knew better. Still to this day I have family members that kill for pay. There have been some very famous unsolved murders that I know for sure my family is responsible for. We ask God to forgive us, and He does. Not only do we just pray, but we always give Him a portion of our profit."

By the end of his speech I was speechless. He told his family history as if it was normal to kill people. I watched his hands to make sure he didn't reach for a gun or anything since he'd just let me in on so much. My heart was beating fast. It almost felt like it was ready to jump out of my body.

"Relax Mo. I won't ever hurt you or my kids. Especially not Denise."

It was like a light bulb went off in my head. "The girl. Your, I don't know what she'd be to you, but the girl. Whoever has the girl has the power?" I felt that in my chest. "You used me?" I hopped down from the bed, taking the sheet with me.

Senior met me at the door. "No! Yes, I mean no!" He shook his head. "Damn Morray!" He kissed his teeth, trying to figure out how he let himself spill out so much, but it was too late. I pushed him out of the way and opened the door to leave out.

Come to think of it, there were no other women in his family besides his mother and his aunt who I knew for sure had married into the family. It all made sense now. My child was *The Martin.*

When I got back to the room, Denise was still sleeping, but that was about to change. We were leaving. I wasn't staying here with a man whose linage was murderous. I damn for sure wasn't going to sleep in the house with him.

"I can't let you leave." Senior closed the door behind him as he came in my room.

"So you've told me now you have to kill me?" I threw the bag on the bed and folded my arms. "I'm not going to tell anyone, but I can't stay here knowing that you never loved me, but I was all a part of your plan."

"See this is why I didn't want to tell you. I don't think you'd snitch on me, but I can't let you go. Morray I could've gotten a daughter out of any broad, but I wanted you. I wanted you to be my wife." He started moving closer and I got scared, so I picked up Denise. He for sure wasn't going to hurt me if I had her in my arms.

"Get back Senior!" I held my hand out so he didn't get too close. The situation probably looked weird if someone would walk in. We were both naked!

"I'm not going to do you anything. Damn Morray! Get that through your head. I really do love you. Geneva doesn't even know all of this, but you do. Hell, her own family is involved and I never told her any of this. How do you think I can afford all of this? The church? My family doesn't take a penny from the church besides love gifts." This was becoming too much. Now I wished I would've walked away when I first had the chance, but I was a day late and a dollar short of that. I felt light headed, so I took a seat on the bed and held tight onto Denise. Senior rested his back against the wall and let me have my space and time, but he wasn't leaving.

"Does David know?" Senior shook his head from side to side. "Why?"

"Because my uncle who controlled everything before I came into power had a feeling that David Jr. wasn't mine so I wasn't at liberty to include him yet. Now that I have that power, he wants nothing to do with me." He was chewing on his bottom lip as if he was as nervous as I was.

Now that I knew everything, I still felt as though I was lost. I knew for sure that there was no getting out now. I had my daughter, and even if she brought him power, she brought me life. I was going to do what was best for her and I know taking her away from her family wasn't the best.

"After you die what happens? She's the only girl." I looked down at my beautiful daughter who'd fallen asleep again.

"You're my wife. Everything if yours because you gave me the girl."

Now I felt as though I was a part of the mafia or something. I didn't know anything about killing people. Heck I didn't know too much about being a first lady of somebody's church. There was no way that was going to become my responsibility. I didn't even want Denise knowing any of this stuff.

"That won't happen." I shook my head and turned my body on the bed.

Senior came closer to me and I eyed him because I still wasn't trying to be friendly with him. I was just trying to get a better understanding. "Relax, I'm just sitting down." He moved himself down to the foot of the bed to put some space in between us.

"You kind of don't have a choice. You're my wife. I know it may seem like a lot right now, but just give it some time."

I still had another question. I wasn't getting over it that easily. "But why me Senior? Did I look weak or something? Was I an easy target? Did I look like I didn't have any self-esteem?" Senior shook his head *no* to all of my questions. "Then what was it?"

"When I saw those pictures in DJ's phone, something about you made me feel like I had get you. Since the day I laid eyes on you for the first time at the church, you had been on my mind and those pictures sealed the deal. Yes, I figured you'd give me a baby, but I didn't think I would love you as much as I do. I know it was wrong to take you from my son, but I felt like you were my soulmate and I wasn't going to risk not finding out. Maybe I could've went about it differently, but I'm glad I did what I did."

I sat there and listen to what he said, but I prayed to God that He didn't hold me accountable for the actions of my child's father.

Chapter Twenty-One
Pastor David

Since I had a chance to clear my chest to my wife, I felt so much better. It was as if a weight was lifted off of me having been able to let someone else in on my secret life. Nobody outside of my family knew the truth, not even the people of the church knew. Although Geneva had an idea that our families had history, she didn't know everything. She wasn't strong enough, and was simply chosen because of her suspected fertility.

Six days had gone by since I had bared it all, and Morray was still acting strange. Not saying that I didn't understand why, but six days later I did expect her to be over it. She didn't think I knew it, but she slept with a gun under her mattress. That was a shocker to me because I told her she didn't have to worry about me ever hurting her. I loved her almost as much as I loved Denise. No I may not act like it, but I'm just letting it be known.

Today was going to be different, it had better be different. Today was the day that Denise was going to be Christened and dedicated back to The Lord. I had family coming from all across the country just for this occasion. Well that was not the only reason, but today was also the day that I was going to officially be sworn in as *The Mfalme*. I never really understood why my family always wanted to keep the Swahilian translation instead of calling the head of the family a king, but whatever it was, it was who I was going to be.

I'd hired a chef for the day. There was to be a grand party after church after in our backyard. People were running around my house like mad dogs because Helena hired a party planner to execute her vision with perfection, or at least that's what she'd told Morray over the phone.

It took me no time to get ready leaving me to have time to spend with Denise. She was sitting in her mother's room with her two aunts while Morray was being dolled up with the make-up artist and hairstylist I'd hired for her. I spoke to Kedra and Helena before going into the bathroom to peek at my wife.

"You need something Senior?" Morray looked at me through the mirror as the woman applied some powder to her cheekbones, and just as she had done for the past few days, she turned her head around and scanned the entire room before

looking straight ahead again.

"Morray you damn near made me mess up with this

bronzer. Stay still!" The woman doing her make-up threw the

brush down and put her hands on her hips, but Morray shrugged

her shoulders and turned her attention back to me.

"No, I was just coming to see how everything was coming

along. You know church starts in an hour?" I looked down at my

Apple watch to make sure I was correct.

Helena came into the bathroom with Denise on her hip.

She was Morray's ghetto friend, and honestly, I didn't care too

much for her. The only reason why I agreed to allow her to be

Denise's godmother was because she and her husband have been

having a hard time conceiving.

"David, you can get out. No men are allowed. You

weren't worried about Morray all of two months ago, don't start

now. Denise tell Daddy bye-bye." She waved at me and of course

my daughter followed suit.

Kayla Andrè

I wasn't worried about Helena kicking me out of any room of my house, and neither was Morray. "Helena be nice," she laughed, but I she bit her bottom lip. I know that she has told Helena everything and was worried that her best friend may say more. "Senior I know what time church starts. Angela is almost finished my hair and my face is done. Denise's dress is on the bed and she's had a bath and all. Can you go make sure they've sent the trailers with the restrooms to the back of the house please? Absolutely no one is to be inside of this house during the party."

"Yea, but don't forget I have a family meeting tonight that you must attend." Her phone started to ring so she dismissed me by the flick of her wrist. "See you in a few Baby Girl," I kissed Denise's forehead on the way out.

It would've been too much like right if we would've made it to church on time. Not that we were too late, but we were late enough. Thankfully my church knows to start without me. I may be the pastor, but they have lives of their own and don't need t be in church all day because my wife had booked a photographer and wanted to take pictures at the last minute.

The entire service I watched as my family all sat in one section, including Morray's family and my son. The front section of the church was full, and it seem like we were getting even more members because the terrace section didn't look as scattered as it had in the past.

After my sermon, it was time for the Christening. Troy had to perform the ceremony since it was my child. Dean and Helena came up to the front and took the vow to have active rolls in Denise's life and to make sure that she was properly taken care of also meaning that they would walk with her in her Christian journey.

There were so many flashes coming from all different directions that I almost thought that I was on a red carpet. Denise loved the attention she was receiving. She hadn't cried all service and didn't even want her pacifier. She sat on her grandmother's lap during the service and when it was time to go before the church she wore the biggest smile, as if she knew what was

happening.

"Denise must think she's famous." Morray laughed at

Denise as she sat in her car seat holding my phone. The camera

app was open, and she was staring at herself. Denise looked up at

her mom and smiled. "Yea, I'm talking about you little girl."

There was a pain in my chest seeing them interact.

Knowing that I'll never have that with Denise, hurt. I would not

be there to walk her down the aisle. I wouldn't even be there for

her first day at school. Denise won't even know who her father

was, but that was aching me more than the thought of death.

When the limousine pulled in front of the house, Morray

got out and I got Denise and myself out. "Can I talk to you for a

minute before we go inside?" People were already arriving for

the party, passing by with their gifts in hand. I didn't want

anyone in our business so I figured I should make the

conversation a fast one.

We stood at our front door since nobody was allowed

inside. I checked around before I started to speak. "Look, I know

I was never the best husband to you. No amount of money I

threw your way could make up for the things I put you through.

Between trying to blackmail you, uprooting your life, and then

being sent to prison for so long. You didn't deserve that, you are

a good woman. After I die, I know you may not want to, but

please help with my family business. Troy can handle a lot, but

you are on my accounts. He can't access most of them without

you. I emailed my last will and testament to my lawyer this

morning, and I'm leaving you everything, but I did set up a trust

for DJ.

I now know that you were never for me, but you were for

him. He may not come here today or even my funeral, but I do

want him to have a successful life. The church is going to vote in

Troy as their pastor, but until he finds a wife, you still should

attend."

Morray's face was emotionless as I confided in her as

well as apologized. I was just about to shut my mouth and allow

her to enjoy her day until I saw a tear roll down her cheek.

Denise was in my arms, but when she saw her mother crying she reached for her. Denise tried to take her hand and catch the tears, but that made Morray laugh.

"Senior, I do have love for you, and at some point, I did want us to work. Hopefully God performs a miracle, and He spares your life because you are being a good father to Denise. I forgive you for everything, but I know I'm not the only person you should be apologizing to." She was talking about DJ, but I wasn't stressing behind that because the possibility of him wanting to talk to me was slim to none.

We stood in an awkward silence for a brief moment until the party planner opened the front door and said that Morray needed to get in so Denise could change. It was about time for me to come out of this suit with the sun beaming down the way it was.

The backyard was packed with everyone who was trying to be seen and experience a Martin pool party. I don't even want to look at the bill when it comes because all of the decorations and rented party supplies had me expecting the worse. There was

Ferris wheel, a petting zoo, a concession stand, two inflatable

waterslides, and about three bounce houses.

"Son," my mother called me over to her. She was sitting

at a table alone, but that wasn't surprising. "Mayor Douglas came

by the house the other day to inform me about the verbal

agreement we have."

Although I was told everything was squared away, I knew

that if it wasn't done the way my mother would want it, then it

had to be redone. That was another reason why I couldn't wait to

make this reign official. I was tired of answering to her. Even

with death being near, I still wanted to create a legacy in

whatever amount of time I had.

When she stopped talking, I nodded my head for her to

continue. "I'm very proud in the way you executed all of this

from behind bars. Your brother, Solomon, is over there with

Troy. They are supposed to be discussing the 2020 presidential

election. We're looking at a congressman from Delaware, but he

needs work."

Kayla Andrè

I wanted so badly to tell her I wasn't going to be here so it wasn't my problem, but I knew that meant not being able to receive what was rightfully mine. "Yes ma'am? Where are my other two brothers?"

My mother scanned the party and laughed. "They are over there committing one of the seven deadly sins. You'd think they would ask God to forgive them so they could lose some weight." She picked up her strawberry and took a bite before proceeding. "I see that wife of yours is losing weight. Maybe she's understanding what it means to be in this family or maybe it's your son getting ahold of her."

"How do you know about that?" I stood up from the table. I wasn't angry, but I was concerned. My mother didn't bother with me unless it had to deal with the family business, so I didn't understand how she knew my personal business.

"I know everything David. I know everything." She looked back at the party and smiled. All I could do was shake my head because I wasn't sure what else she thought she knew.

The Other Side Of The Pastor's Bed 3

For three hours, I pretended to enjoy my daughter's party. Socializing with family and friends was something that I hadn't done in many years, but the time had come for my induction. Morray didn't know what she was getting into, and I could tell she was nervous when we entered my office and the room was filled with the men of my family and my mom. I had Denise in one hand while Morray was holding the other. She held onto my hand so tight that when she did finally let go, I realized it had fallen asleep. I hated that she had to be a part of this because it wasn't normal, but it was my normal.

"You ready?" My brother Solomon asked me. Once I gave him the green light, the room stood still. "May all heads bow and all eyes be closed. Dear God, we gather before you today asking you to anoint the fifth generation mfalme in your blood so that he can lead this family to greatness. We ask that any sin he has to commit in order to sustain this family be washed away in the blood of Jesus and be forgiven. Shall any man rise against him, may they shall fall in the pits of Hell and you show them no mercy.

Kayla Andrè

Thank you God for blessing David with a precious daughter and because he was the only one in the family able to produce a girl, we know you have designed him just for this task. As a unit, he and his wife were chosen and given Denise who you placed on Earth as an angel. May our ancestors give us their spiritual power to continue this bloodline. In Jesus name, we pray. Amen."

What was coming next was going to give Morray a heart attack, but I looked over to her and kissed her to distract her from what was happening. Although she wasn't receptive to the kiss at first, she opened her mouth once I placed my hand on her behind. Denise's scream let me know that the step had been completed.

"This is the blood of the only pure soul we have in our bloodline. With this blood, my brother, Pastor David will be made whole again." He pressed down on Denise's foot to get more blood to drip into the wine glass. "Morray?"

I knew Morray didn't want to embarrass me and I also knew that I probably should've warned her that she was going to have to give up blood, but I knew that would only cause problems that I didn't want to deal with. If looks could kill, I would have been in the ground by the way Morray sliced her eyes at me.

"Your hand?" My brother asked. Morray hesitantly gave him her hand. He took the same knife he'd cut Denise's foot with and cut the tip of Morray's finger. She kept her eyes on me the entire time. The droplets of blood were heard going into the glass of wine. "The blood of his wife is going to give him the spirit of discernment that God has given her."

Lastly, it was my turn. Reaching out my hand, I felt the dull pain of my skin opening, but it had to be done. Once all three of bloods were mixed within the wine it was time for me to drink. I had to drink the entire glass or none of the blessings would come to me.

"May God continue to bless you, my brother." Solomon started a slow clap once I placed the empty glass onto the desk. The room was cheerful with everyone wishing their blessings upon me.

Everyone came to the front to hug their new king and surprisingly my wife stayed by my side although Denise was taken by Solomon. He was a doctor and wanted to make sure her foot would be ok. Which I was sure it would because my family had been doing this for generations.

Once the room was cleared, Morray followed behind them to lock the door. I was prepared for an argument, but I was not prepared to have her hit me upside my head. "Don't you ever in your life subject myself or my child to this satanic bull-crap. Got them cutting my child with a damn knife on her foot. What in the hell is wrong with you? This is something I should have known about." She took the glass and slammed it to the floor.

I let her vent because I know this was strange to her, but it was done and over with now. There was no turning back. I was the king, and she was my queen rather she wanted to believe it or not. Little did she know that the process wasn't over.

"Talk to me! I know you hear me talking to you." She screamed in my face. Yea, I knew she was angry, but that comes with the territory. I was sure my uncle's wife gave him the same

problems when he took over.

"The process isn't over." I smirked, pulling her close to

me.

"Senior, stop playing with me." She tried to pull away

from me, but I held her tight. "Let me go. I'm going to get my

child."

"Morray, look at me." I was starting to get annoyed by

her little charade. "Look at me, dammit. I'm doing this for

Denise. Denise will never have to work a day in her life and

neither will you. Think about Denise."

"I am thinking about her, but you can't keep doing this.

How do you apologize and then go back and do something like

this?" She'd finally stopped fighting me, but she was looking up

at the ceiling.

I took my hand to her chin and brought her eyes to meet

mine. "I'll call the doctor to have the surgery if you finish this

process. My family is waiting. They may not be behind that door,

but I know they are waiting."

Kayla Andrè

"What's the process Senior? Because this is becoming too much."

"I couldn't take your bone, but I did take your blood. Now our flesh has to become one." I pulled the sting that was holding her bikini top together, letting it fall and reveal her full breasts. "I promise you that it won't be long."

Her nostrils flared as she gazed at me. Yea I knew she was about done with me, and probably wanted to tell me not to get the surgery. She looked around the room as she thought to herself. "I'm not having sex in here."

She walked away before I could say anything. Tying her bikini up as she walked out of the office. Thankfully nobody was in the house and I could give Morray my best once more because I was sure this time was going to be our last.

When we got up to the room, she undressed herself and laid back on the bed with her legs open. She looked out the window as she waited for me. Undressing myself, I climbed in between her legs for foreplay, but my tongue wasn't even out my mouth before she told me that part wouldn't be necessary.

"There, it should be lubricated enough." She licked the tips of her fingers and transferred the saliva to her womanhood.

Sliding inside of her didn't even feel the same. Usually Morray would be so into the love making that her moans alone would make me climax, but this time she was silent. I knew it felt good to her because there were times she closed her eyes, but she'd turn her head in the opposite direction and open her eyes. I tired kissing her neck, but she moved her shoulders up so that I couldn't get to it anymore. After a while, I gave up. All I needed was to release myself inside of her. She didn't know, but my brother was waiting outside of the door waiting to come in and see that inside of her was where I left myself.

Once I was finished, I threw her a towel. "Cover the top of you. Solomon has to check."

Morray nodded her head, covering the top of herself. I picked my boxers off the floor so I could be covered before my brother came in. "I'm sorry Morray." I tried to kiss her, but she pushed me away and pulled the towel up even more.

Kayla Andrè

Solomon was standing on the other side of the hall when I opened the door. He walked in the room with gloves on his hand. Morray already was ready when he walked up. Her legs were propped open. "How are you feeling?"

"Don't act like this is cool because it's not. Do what you have to do, and then leave." Morray kissed her teeth. My brother turned to look at me, but I didn't have anything to say.

He stuck two fingers inside of her and felt around before bringing them back out. He took his thumb and rubbed the substance around for a little bit. "Well brother, you are officially our king. May your reign be long and prosperous."

Chapter Twenty-Two

First Lady Morray

The disdain I had for Senior was seeping from my pores. I wanted to stab him in the back of his neck just to prove a point. Thankfully, God was already handling him for me. My skin was crawling with the disappointment I had for myself. I didn't have to have sex with him. I could have put up more of a fight, but I just wanted to ensure my child to have a better life than I even could imagine possible.

Now as for his baldheaded brother, Solomon, coming in after we had sex and practically fingering me in order to retrieve the semen out of my body, I wanted to start a fire. There was nothing left for me to say to Senior. Yes, I was still at the house, but I had made a promise to my daughter that she would spend Senior's last moments on Earth living with him, and although she may not understand, I was not going back on my word to her.

Senior had called the doctor to schedule the surgery and today we were going to the hospital to pre-register. Yes, I did say *we*. Call me weak or whatever names you want, but I was just keeping my word. Hopefully the surgery did to him what he feared it would and he still leaves this Earth.

"So are you brining Denise or what?" My mother pried into my business during our Facetime call. She and my father had gone home the day after everything, but she was already talking about coming back. "You know if I was there you wouldn't have to bring her to that dirty hospital."

I continued to get Denise dressed while my mother continued to run her mouth. She should've known better than to think I was going to bring Denise to the hospital. Helena was coming by in a few minutes to get Denise to go to the zoo with Kedra and her girls.

"I had a chance to speak with your mother-in-law at the party. She said you and Senior were having problems. Why didn't you tell me?" The question was so idiotic that I had to stop in the middle of placing on Denise's shoes.

With the phone in my hand so she could see me, I rolled my eyes. "Mother, you were here when they arrested my husband in our home. You were here for the problems." I threw the phone

back down when Helena's text came through saying she was at

the gate. "Besides, I know what you're doing Mom. No, I'm not

coming home. You've been counting on my marriage to fail ever

since I got married." There was no way I was going to actually

tell her that she was right and that I had gotten in over my head,

but it was what is was.

After getting Denise's shoes on her, I threw her diaper

bag on my shoulder and headed downstairs to let my best friend

in. "No Morray, that is not what I meant, but you know your

father and I are here if you decide to divorce him and marry

someone your own age."

My mother always made it hard not to be disrespectful.

Nothing I ever did was good enough for her so there was no

reason for to try and convince her that I wasn't failing in my

marriage because if I had my way she would never know.

"Yes ma'am, but Helena is here so I'll call you later. I

love you, and tell Daddy I said hi." I kissed the camera and told

Denise to wave before I hung up and stuck the phone in my

pocket.

By the time I made it to the door, Helena was already

calling my phone trying to get in. I knew she hadn't been at the

door long, but she was impatient. "Here, take her and leave."

Helena pushed me aside and made her way into the house.

"Girl please. I know you are not giving her up that easily." She

showed me to the kitchen as if we were in her house. "Hey

Nanny!" She looked back at Denise as she reached in the fridge

and pulled out a bottle of water.

"How are you going to come in my house like it's yours?"

I rolled my eyes, playfully. I sat Denise on the island so that I

could get the heavy diaper bag off of my shoulder. "Anyways, I

may meet up with y'all after I leave from with him?"

My best friend nodded her head while looking around the

kitchen. "So how is everything going with you know what?" She

wasn't trying to say the words because who knew if Senior was

listening or not.

"Yea, I went talked to the man yesterday after my nail appointment. Everything is good," I plastered a smile on my face so that she knew that I was ok.

Helena studied me for a moment, waiting for me to crack, but I wasn't. At least not in front of her. She still didn't know what happened at the party when we disappeared for an hour, but I came up with a lie saying we had to handle something with the church. I was sure she knew I was lying, but she went along with it.

"Ok. Well, let's get going Nanny. Kedra should almost be at the zoo. Call me when you leave." She grabbed Denise and the diaper bag before she left out of the door.

I sent a text to Senior to let him know that I was downstairs and ready to leave. We had to be at the hospital for noon and it was already eleven-thirty. As I waited for him to come down, I went to get my purse out of the den where I left it the day before. The sound of the news caught my attention. I didn't always watch the news, but I guess Senior was down here this morning.

Kayla Andrè

"Police are trying to find a woman who went missing from her home in the 4600 block of Pelican Bay Drive. Sources say the last time they heard from Liana Marvin was about two weeks ago, when she announced to a neighbor that was expecting a child.

There isn't a reason to suspect foul play, but the woman's family says there would be no reason for her to go leave town without at least letting someone know. If you have any information about the missing person in this case, please call your local prescient to report it. "

"I told you she was going to get handled for what she'd done to our daughter. There was no way she wasn't going to pay for her actions." Senior crept up behind me, making me jump since I wasn't expecting him to be there.

Although I said I wanted to stomp her in the dirt, and I knew about his family history, I never expected him to have her killed. "She's dead?" I turned off the television and picked up my purse, trying to stop myself from thinking.

"Don't be like that. I told you about me and what I do. No I didn't do this myself, but yes Mo, she is dead." His voice rose just a little, and that made me snap my neck in his direction. "I'm not yelling, but aren't you happy? Isn't this better than sending her to jail where she could get out?" One would really forget this man was a pastor. He for sure didn't act like one in private, and sometimes public.

God please forgive me for whatever hand I had in this, I said a quick prayer and did the sign of the cross as I made my way to the door. The conversation was over because I didn't want to know any more information that could possibly send me to jail.

The ride to the hospital was so quiet that I'd forgotten that I wasn't alone in the car. I liked the quietness, but of course Senior wanted to start some sort of conversation as if he and I were on good terms.

Kayla Andrè

"How does it feel to be driving a Bentley SUV? When I traded in your old SUV, I knew you would love this one." He looked around the car, proud of himself. "You like the color?"

The more he talked the sicker I became. "It's a damn gold Bentley. I was fine with my Audi. You took it upon yourself to trade my car in, without my permission." I rolled my eyes and turned into the parking lot.

"Well I figured we could match. His and Her Bentley's." He smiled at me and had the nerve to place his hand on my thigh.

He'd lost his mind. It had to be the cancer or something, because there was no way he thought I would be ok. "Senior, stop it now! Leave me alone, and keep your hands to yourself. We will never go back to that anymore."

I'd had it with him. I parked in the first spot I saw, and turned the car off. I was feeling queasy and I was sure it was because of my soon-to-be deceased husband. My phone started to vibrate in my back pocket. Pulling it out, I saw it was David, so I answered.

"We need to talk. I need you home. I'm not going to keep doing this with you. We're either going to stay together or we aren't, but I know with me is where you want to be. I don't care what happened while you were at that man's house, but we are starting over. I'm sorry for what I said, but I want to be with you. I want to be with you and Denise. You all are my family; all I have. I love you, Morray."

While David was on the phone with me, his father was standing by my side trying to get my attention. My mouth started to feel watery and my eyes felt like I was about to cry. There was no stopping it from coming. I snatched my phone away from my ear and spilled my guts onto the concrete.

"What the hell Mo?" Senior jumped back and it just missed him. "Hold on. Let me get you a napkin from the car."

David was calling my name loud enough for me to hear without having the phone next to my ear, and it wasn't on speaker. "Yea. I just threw up." I took the napkin from Senior and wiped my mouth before throwing the napkin in the vomit.

Kayla Andrè

Stepping around it, I told Senior I would meet him upstairs, but I was going to the Ladies Room. "Morray are you sick or something?" David wondered as I rinsed my mouth out with the faucet water.

"No. It probably was because of the car ride or something. Back to what you were saying." I fixed myself in the mirror, trying to make sure my make-up wasn't messed up. "I love you too David. I'm getting some things together to ensure that you and I can be together."

"Like what Morray. I don't want you changing when you are around him. Wearing your ring because you're going to see him at the church is too much. If you're done, then be done. I'm ready to commit myself to you. I need to know you're willing to do the same."

This felt like a movie because normally people didn't end up with the person who they wanted to be with. Especially when they'd gone through everything David and I had been through. I loved him, and I was grateful he loved me the same.

"I am willing, Bae. It's us against the world!"

"Then act like it, and bring that behind here to Daddy."

"Soon, Daddy. Very soon."

"Don't take too long girl." We both laughed, and it felt good. After the arguing and the crying, it felt good to laugh with the person my heart yearned for. Thinking on the two times I had sex with his father made me scared. I didn't know what would happen if David found out nor was I trying to see.

Women were starting to come into the bathroom so I told David I would call him back once I left from where I was. By the time I'd made it up to the area where Senior was supposed to be, he was being called to the back by a doctor. That had us both confused because you never saw a doctor when you pre-registered. It was always blood work and talking to the nurse at the counter.

When in the room, the doctor asked me to close the door behind us. Senior and I both looked over at each other trying to figure out what it could be. I took my seat and waited. I wasn't going to say a prayer because it could be that this man was going to leave me sooner than later, and that was fine with me.

Kayla Andrè

"I know you both are confused as to why I called you in here. First, my name is Dr. Kumari, and I am the lead surgeon at this hospital. Mr. Martin, I called you in today because your primary doctor has been under investigation for a scam he was doing. He's been performing surgeries on a number for patients, claiming they had a tumor in their lung.

These x-rays he showed you were the same set he used with every patient. He would go in saying he was removing the tumor, but he was just make unnecessary incisions. I know we should have caught on to it a long time ago, but he was working with a team of nurses so no one was suspicious. After the fifth patient, the hospital became alarmed. I'm sorry for the inconvenience this has caused you and your family. On behalf of the hospital, I am willing to offer you some form of restitution"

A lump was stuck in my throat and I didn't know if I was happy or sad. Hell, I don't even know if I was understanding completely. "I don't have cancer?" Senior asked, just as confused as I was.

"No Sir. You are not going to die in six weeks. That was his story with every patient he spoke to." Dr. Kumari smiled, but I was dying. I just knew I was going to get over with this marriage.

Senior grabbed my hand and started to swing it, happily. "Mo, I'm not dying! I'm here forever, Baby!"

I gritted my teeth and tried to force a smile to come. "So why did he faint that day? What's wrong with him?" Giving Senior a glance over, I was sure something was wrong.

"I'm not sure. I'll have to run some tests, but I can assure you that you won't be dying of cancer." Senior was so excited, but I was hurt. My feelings were hurt, and I didn't want to do what I had to do.

As Senior and the doctor continued to discuss the misdiagnosis, I took my phone out and sent a text to the number I had saved under *Help*, then I just sat back in my chair and waited for the conversation to be over with. If God wasn't going to get me out of this shell of a marriage, I would get myself out.

Kayla Andrè

After an hour, we were on our way out of the hospital and there was somebody waiting by my car. I knew what they were there for once I saw the envelope. I detoured to the restroom just so I didn't have to witness it.

I waited exactly ten minutes before going back out. Senior was standing by the car looking over the papers when I walked up. He looked over at me and shook his head. "You couldn't even wait, huh? This is crazy." He was more so speaking to himself than he was to me.

Senior knew it was coming, and I didn't know why he was acting so surprise. Even inside the car, he still was mumbling. I continued to drive and pray that he didn't try to hurt me. "A damn divorce Morray? A divorce?"

He was truly acting as if this was coming out the wazoo. "Yes Senior, a divorce. Sign it so we can both move on. It wasn't a secret that I haven't been happy in this marriage, and neither have you or else you would've never strayed from me. You chose to sleep with that woman."

The Other Side Of The Pastor's Bed 3

Since he didn't have anything else to say, I figured the conversation was over. I was wrong because when we stepped inside of the house, he started again. Asking me why I didn't want to make this marriage work. There was no way he was being serious. Why would I want to do that?

I stood in the kitchen as he sat down at the island with the papers in front of him, turning from page to page trying to find something else to complain or whine about. "Senior stop! We are not going to act like this is just something that I pulled from a branch on a tree. You know why we are here. You are why we are here. The day you whipped your penis out and for that woman, you decided we would end here. It's my fault too because how could I expect you to do right by me when you slept with me, knowing I was with your teenage son.

As much as I tried to put everything behind us for the sake of Denise, I can't. The image of you having sex with her won't leave my head. What you thought I didn't know? I followed you Senior. I do my research, and you might want to make sure your sidelines aren't scared of a beat down because it didn't take too much for her to tell my P.I. about when everything started." My heart was pumping fast and I was breathing even harder.

"You put me through so much, and I'll never be able to recover from this relationship. I hate you. I wanted you gone, but no you just had to have a miracle. You are a liar, and the truth isn't in you. You and your family believe that by saying your prayers and asking God to forgive you makes everything ok, but it doesn't. Y'all are going to Hell. I promise you that."

Just like I thought. He wasn't saying anything now that I was showing my behind. I was throwing objects left and right, yelling at the top of my voice, and getting in his face. I was tired of him, and all of this. Now that he'd been served, I was free to go.

While in the restroom, I texted Helena and David to let them know that if they hadn't heard from me in an hour, to call the police. I had thirty minutes left before my time was up. I walked out of the kitchen and up to my room.

Most of Denise's things were packed inside of two duffle bags on the bed. I'd placed my bags in the car last night. I threw both bags on my shoulder and reached under my mattress for the gun I started keeping for safety.

My heart was beating fast as I went back down the stairs. I took the gun off safety, and made my way back to the kitchen to get my phone. Of course, I pulled a dumb move and left it on the kitchen counter.

Senior was now standing up, and the papers were still in the same spot. "Don't come close to me."

He held up his hands and stopped only about three feet away from me. I kept the gun aimed at him, and I grabbed my phone and my keys that I didn't know I'd left as well. Senior laughed at me, but I was serious. Him laughing made me a little scared.

"There are no bullets in that gun. I removed them long ago. If you would've let me teach you about guns, you would've been able to tell." He put his arms down and walked back to his seat. "I won't ever hurt you, Mo. You want a divorce, I'll grant you that. God spoke to me. I don't deserve you. I shall spend the rest of my days a single man."

I was starting to think that the God he spoke to and the God I spoke to were two different Gods, but I wasn't trying to find out. I slowly backed out of the kitchen, gun still aimed at him. He could've been lying as far as I was concerned.

"Put the gun down. You're getting your divorce so you can go molest my son. I'll have Jameson look over this and get back with your lawyer. Just leave my house."

Although I wanted to remind him that my name was still on this house and everything else, I didn't. I ran out of that house faster than I'd ran in my entire life. I was happy to be out of here. When I got in the car, I started it and backed out. I didn't wait for the gate to completely open. I knew Senior was crazy, and I was just trying to spare my life.

Twenty-Three
David Jr.

I didn't know why I even told her she could come over, but I felt bad for Kimora. She'd been searching for her mom for three

3 weeks and nothing was coming up. Nobody knew anything either. The neighbor that was the last to see Liana alive said she saw my mom over there a few days before Liana went missing, and that messed me up in the head. I always had my doubts about my mother really being dead, but actually knowing that she wasn't, tripped me out.

While Kimora was worried about tracking her mom down, I was trying to see if she knew my mother was back and where she could've been. "And you say you haven't seen my mother, but your mom told you that she stopped by the house? Did your mom tell you or are you saying that because the neighbor said it?"

"I don't know DJ, damn. Forget her. My mom hasn't been seen in about a month and I don't even know where to look. I have a newborn baby at home, and a missing mother. You think I'm concerned about your whoreish mother?" Kimora dropped her head in her lap. I stood over her, trying to figure out if I wanted to kick her out of my house or not, but I decided against it.

Hopefully she found her mother soon, but I was starting to wonder why my mother was supposedly alive and never reached out to me. Now that I had a child in this world and I was acting like a farther to Denise, I don't see myself doing something like that.

Kimora was still zoned out, trying to get herself together so I left her in the living room so I could go fix me a drink. On my way to the kitchen, I heard someone at the door and I knew it was Morray. I was looking like Mr. Crabs in the meme because it had totally slipped my mind to call my girl and let her know my ex-girl was at my house only because she needed a shoulder to cry on. Me knowing Morray, I knew she was not going to care about any of that.

I met her by the door. She'd been sick and tired the last few weeks, so it was amazing to see her smiling. Denise was on her hip and she had the phone to her ear. I kissed her, but I was trying to block her from going further into the house.

"David move," she tried to step around me, but I blocked her again.

"Wait, let me tell you something?" I whispered, looking back to make sure she couldn't see Kimora sitting on sofa.

Morray looked at me sideways and told whoever she was on the phone with that she would call them back. I'd told Kimora to park on the other side of the street so that Morray didn't see her car near our house.

"Kimora is here, but only because I'm trying to help her find her mom." I took Denise out of her hands so that way she couldn't kill me.

She didn't say anything, but looked around me to see if she could see. "Ok. Now tell her she has to go home." Now I was confused because she said it calmly. I was expecting her to kick and hit me, but she didn't.

Not wanting to provoke her, I nodded my head and walked back to the front. Kimora was texting on her phone, relaxing as if she were comfortable. "Ki, Morray is home and you have to leave."

Denise was still in my arms, looking. You would think that she knew what was going on by the way she was staring. Kimora looked up at me and started to laugh.

"You're going to let her kick me out of your house? That's weak of you. You know I need you right now." She anxiously stood up and grabbed her purse.

It was comical to see her throw herself around because she was mad, but this was the same woman who slept with my best friend, had a baby a tried to pin it on me, and she poisoned me. Not to even mention the fact that she was my sister. This entire dynamic was sick.

"Kimora, get out, please. This is Morray's house too, and I'm asking you to leave." I stepped back so I wasn't blocking her exit. I saw Morray standing at the end of the stairs, waiting for her to leave.

She folded her arms and came stood in front of me. Kimora brought her eyes down upon Denise, but the baby looked away from her. Laughing, she looked over at Morray and then back to me. "I bet her stuff will never be as wet as mine."

That was it. Now I wanted her to go myself. Forget her mother, I don't wish Liana ill, but her child was a different story. "Get the hell out. You're my sister." I pointed at the door so she knew where she needed to walk through.

Just as she was passing Morray, she whispered something I couldn't hear, but Morray grabbed her by her ponytail and pulled her back against the stairwell railing. "Little girl, make this the last time I ever have to see you with your disrespectful tail. Next time, it's on site."

Once she let her go, Morray stepped back as we watched Kimora leave our home. I knew I was going to have to answer a line of questions, so I prepared myself mentally. Denise was pulling at my chin to get my attention. I never knew how much work it would be to have a baby in the home.

"You good Niecey?" I smiled down at her. She moved over mouth around trying to put her lips together to say her favorite word.

"No," she waited for me to pretend to be sad before she started laughing. It was a cute game to play with her. She loved for someone to act as if she'd hurt their feelings.

Morray locked the door and walked to the end of the hall where her daughter and I were standing. Her face showed no emotion so I didn't know which angle she was going to come at me.

"Look, Babe, I never thought she was going to get disrespectful like that. I was only trying to help her because I know what it's like to possibly lose a mother." She wasn't even listening to me. I don't even think she was looking for an apology.

"David, just don't have her in my house again." She stepped past me to go to the kitchen. Something wasn't right because Morray was already to pop off on me, but I just let it go because if I kept it up, she would tick.

My mother came back to mind and I wanted to see how Morray felt about what I was thinking. I followed her to the kitchen as she took out the things she needed to make dinner. I placed Denise down in her walker that was sitting by the breakfast table.

"Morray, I need to talk to you about something." I sat down at the table and waited for her to acknowledge me.

Once she turned the fire on under the pot of water, she walked over to me and sat down. "What's going on?" She played in Denise's hair while she rested. Even though Denise was able to move around in the walker, she wasn't going too far away from us.

"My mom is still alive. I haven't seen her, but I've heard she's back in town." The more I thought about it, the angrier I got. It still seemed outrageous to me that she was even able to come back after faking her death and I wasn't the first person she wanted to see.

Morray's eyes grew bucked and sat up right in her chair. "How this make you feel?"

"Morray, how would you feel if your mother came back from the grave and the first person she went to see was her gay lover?" The question was rhetorical, but I knew she got the point. "I didn't mean any disrespect, but I just don't get it."

"Honestly, I can't say I'm surprised now that I'm thinking about it." I laughed a little to myself, thinking about all of the times my mother didn't act like a mother should. "I do want to see her though. I need closure."

"You can go in the morning." Morray shrugged her shoulders, trying to be some help to me, but that wasn't going to work.

See Morray and I were official. We were a team, and she was my support system. With everything that I had going on, I knew she would be my strength. "No, I need my family there. We can go in the morning." She just nodded her head and leaned forward to kiss me. Times like this made me forget every wrong she'd done to me.

The next morning arrived quicker than I would have liked, but there was no backing out. The three of us were in the car on away to my old home. I hadn't been there since the day I wanted to take my life. My mind tossed words back and forth as I prepared for the conversation was about to have with my mother.

Although no one really knows how a conversation was going to

go, everyone always made up different scenarios. One thing for

sure, I knew I didn't want her to be a part of my life after this

day. All I was seeking was an apology.

Pulling up to the house you wouldn't think anyone was

staying there if you didn't see the lantern on that rested on the

wall near the door. A Hyundai Sonata was parked in front of the

door, and I was starting to think that maybe someone had brought

the house.

"Did my dad mention that someone had brought this

house?" I looked over at Morray who was buried in her phone.

"No. We don't talk about anything concerning her." She

sat her phone down in the cup holder and turned around to see

what Denise was doing behind her. This car was so high-tech that

I was sure she had some gadget keeping her busy. I'd be lying if I

said I didn't like this better than the Audi.

After I parked my car, I said a quick prayer to myself. It

was now or never. Morray said she and Denise would stay in the car, meaning I had to go in by myself. I had to remind myself that

all I needed to do was place one foot in front of the other to make

it to the door.

I knocked for what seemed to be about five minutes and I

was about to turn away until I heard the lock. When the door

opened, I couldn't believe what was standing in front of me. The

woman who was once so beautiful that her skin radiated, was

now pale with no life in her eyes. Her hair was cut short and it

was sticking up from her head. Her eyes seemed to be bigger than

her face.

"Oh my gosh, David Jr. It's a surprise to see you." She

reached out for a hug, but I was hesitant at first. "My only son."

Having her close to me made me want to puke. She

reeked of cigarette smoke and beer. I followed her inside and I

became more and more upset with each piece of garbage that

rested randomly in the floor. What pissed me off more was seeing

some big, sloppy, man laying down on the sofa with nothing, but

a pair of boxers on while smoking a blunt.

"Oh, so this is our son?" This man had the nerve to refer

to me as son. I was ready to get a gun and light into him, but I

was sure he would only ooze sweet potato pie, and not die.

"Man, shut the hell up, and don't ever fix your lips to

speak to me again." I snapped because in that moment I realized

how far gone my mother was, and now I didn't even know who

she was. In all actuality, I didn't care to.

"Don't talk to my fiancé like that. Respect him." Geneva,

yes Geneva, took the blunt from him and brought it up to her lips.

"The Bible tells us to honor our mothers and our fathers."

The nerve of this woman to tell me anything about The

Bible. "Man don't tell me anything about anything. You are a

sorry excuse for a woman, and damn for sure for a sorry excuse

for a mother. I came here with the idea somewhere in my head

thinking that you were going to apologize to me about you've

treated me, but I'm good. Stay here, looking like a crack head.

I'm going to pray for you."

I turned to walk away, but I felt something hit the back of

my head. This woman was really trying me. Looking down at the floor, I saw it was the television remote. When I turned to confront her, I saw she was halfway to me already.

"I never wanted to have you anyways. You were a mistake, and you ruined my life. You made my husband cheat on me. You took away my figure," she placed her hands on her hips as she yelled in my face.

"Nah, Nene you are still fine!" The husky man spoke up. Geneva started cheesing harder than ever before. I notice her canine tooth was missing.

God really was holding me back because she was no longer a mother to me, but a random woman on the street who needed to be taught a lesson. I wanted to go outside and get my girl to stomp her so badly, but I didn't.

"Whatever you say about me DJ, you come from me so that makes you just like me. It was the best decision I've ever made when I faked my own death. I was away from all of you. God revealed to me that I was greater than the pain y'all put me through. You are sick and are going to hell for having sex with your sister, and I think you should've died in that car crash."

Before I could stop myself, my hand was wrapped around her neck, pushing her up against the wall. I was tired of all of this. How was it that this woman who birthed me could be so evil? The life that I was given nothing, but tests and I was tried. My mind was replaying all of her words, but the phrase that she wanted me to die was speaking the loudest. I was so caught up in my mind that I didn't see Biggie walking up on me. His fist was already colliding with the side of my face by the time I was made aware of his presence.

"Boy leave my girl alone. I'll kill you." He started to punch at me, but missed every time. He was so out of shape that after three punches he needed to catch his breath. I looked back at Geneva as she sat on the floor holding her throat.

"Look, I'm out of here. Forget you and never talk to me or my family again. As far as I'm concerned you died almost a year ago." I was done, and I had nothing left in me. It was like a weight had been lifted from my chest. I didn't hate her, but I was indifferent.

Kayla Andrè

I got back in the truck and drove away. Morray was talking, but I wasn't understanding what she was saying. My mind was so wrapped up in itself that I didn't have a chance to listen to her. My phone ringing was the only thing that snapped me out of it.

"Hello?" I answered without looking at the number.

"Is this David Martin?" I hated when people said that because it made me feel like they were trying to confirm they had their correct target so they could kill me.

"Yes," I replied.

"This is Logan Brady. I'm an assistant coach with the Los Angeles Dodgers. Given your performance here at the tryout, we are looking to offer you a chance to sign with us. We are offering two seasons for eight million dollars."

I pulled the car to the side of the road to make sure I was hearing him correctly. "Did you say eight million dollars?" I just needed to make sure my ears weren't playing tricks on me.

Morray was on the side of me slapping her thighs and cursing, but when I said the eight million dollars out loud, suddenly she wanted to get quiet.

"Yes Sir. We need you out here as soon as possible though. Our lawyers will send you over the contract. We'll set up a flight for you. Is that fine?" He sounded like he thought I would have a problem. Hell, for eight million dollars I was sure to be fine with just about anything.

"That's fine. I'll have my lawyer look over it as well. Thank you."

"Who was that?" Morray wasted no time getting on my case. "And I know you've been hearing me talking this entire time. How did everything go with your mom?"

I was so excited that I got out the car and ran over to the passenger side. I opened Morray's door and told her to get out.

"Boy hell no. We are in the middle of an abandoned parking lot. What is wrong with you? What about that money?"

Luckily for me she didn't have a seatbelt on and I was able to pull her out of the car. "If you would just shut-up I could tell you that I was offered a contract to play for the Los Angeles

Dodgers!" I held her hands in mine.

I was trying to think about if I wanted to do what I what I

told myself I was going to do, but it was now or never. I knew I

loved her and I knew that I wanted her forever.

"Oh my gosh David! Congratulations! I am so proud of

you my love!" Morray was crying with excitement so I knew she

was about to be sobbing when I got down on one knee. "David,

what are you doing?"

Looking up at her, I knew she was my person. The one

God made just for me. I'd never seen anything more beautiful,

and she was just wearing an Adidas sweat suit.

"Morray Elizabeth Harper, the day I first saw you, I

wanted to know more about you. Not just who you were or where

you came from, but I wanted to know what made you laughed. I

wanted to know what made you cry and how you liked your eggs

scrambled. I wanted to know the little things. The things that you

never told to anyone else, I wanted to know.

You've made me the happiest man in my life, and you have also brought me a lot of pain. All of it was worth it because we've made it through the storm. You are my reason for everything I do, and now that I am with you that means I have to be with Denise too, and I love her like she is my own. Will you do me the honor of becoming my wife and keep making me the happiest man on Earth?"

She was backed away from me and started shaking her head. "I have to tell you something."

Honestly, I didn't know if she was crying because she was happy or sad, but I knew I was tired of being on my knee on this concrete. I stood up on my feet, pulling her closer to me, but she tried to back away.

"Morray, what the hell? I just asked you to be my wife and you on this funny stuff. What do you have to tell me?" She was taking so long that I knew Denise was going to wake up from her nap and start crying.

"I'm pregnant." She covered her face in shame. The way she was acting let me know that she didn't know if it were mine.

That hurt me because this would be the second time she's done me down bad. I fought the air because I needed to take my frustration out on something. "Look, we'll figure that out when we can. In the meantime, you have to promise me that this is us. My father is no longer your concern. Yea, he can see Denise, but this is us. Ain't no more back and forth."

Morray started laughing like this was funny, but I wasn't laughing. I wanted to smack that smirk off of her face. "What's so comical?"

"I wanted to see how much you love me. I am pregnant, but I went to the doctor's yesterday. I checked the dates and this is your baby. When I came home yesterday, I was trying to tell you, but you had that trick in my house."

I grabbed her and held her as tightly as I could. "Don't play like that Morray!" I spun her around. "We about to have a baby and you're going to be my wife. Man!"

She grabbed my face and kissed me. "I can't wait! I love you David. We forever?"

"And ever! You just made me the happiest man alive!"

The Other Side Of The Pastor's Bed 3
With everything we had going on and the trials we've

gone through to be together, it was all worth it. Who would've

know that I would go from cleaning my shoeprint off her desktop

to being her husband?

Epilogue
Morray Elizabeth Harper-Martin

Sixteen years had passed since the day David popped the question to me on the side of the road, and it has been a ride ever since them. With David deciding that he wanted to retire from the game and move back to Tampa this year, my life has been crazy. Not to mention I was now the proud owner of *The Plus Size Trophy Wife*. It was my brand and I offered everything from clothing to hair vitamin supplements. Adding in the fact that I was now a mother of four, moving across the country wasn't the easiest thing to do.

"Are you going to allow me to bring him to dinner on Sunday?" Denise asked me for the third time since I'd picked her up from school.

Starring over at her, I couldn't believe that my baby girl was asking me if she could bring a boy to dinner. "I'll have to talk to your farther first."

"Ooooo. Denise has a boyfriend," the twins Dakota and Demi both cooed from the backseat.

Denise melted in her seat, but it was cute to see her slightly blush. "Fine, but make sure you both remember the time when Dad caught Daniel and that girl together."

She always liked to bring that up whenever she thought she would be in trouble or when she wanted to get something she wasn't sure she could have, but little did she know, I've been waiting for her to ask if this little nappy headed boy could come over.

My life was picture perfect now and we'd left all of the drama behind us, and I was no longer finding myself on the other side of the pastor's bed. Now I woke up to my husband, and we didn't have any of the problems that I had with Senior. Not to say we didn't have any problems, but we didn't those problems.

After the divorce, Senior and I agreed to be cordial for the rest of the family. He and Denise we super close. She spends two weeks every summer with him from the time she was a baby. I never had to worry about a wicked step-mother because he never remarried. Actually, he dedicated his life to the church and Denise said he wasn't dating. He had passed down the family business to some nephew who had a daughter about ten years

ago. My other kids didn't know him as grandfather because he

wasn't David's farther. Steven was their grand farther and Kedra

was their Auntie Nana.

"Denise wants her boyfriend to come to dinner on

Sunday. I was thinking it would a good idea." I laid on my

husband's chest after hopping off of his member and preparing to

go to sleep.

David started laughing, making me rise my head to look

at him. "Don't look at me like that, but it's crazy to me that the

same baby that used to stick Cheetos in her nose wants to date

someone."

"Boy leave my baby alone, but anyways, she did bring up

the situation with Daniel and that does have some validity. You

caught him having sex last month, in our house, and you didn't

cut up at all; it was me."

David nodded his head because he knew it was true, but

that didn't make him right. I was ready to beat all the black off of

my son's skin when I got home, but his farther wasn't as upset.

What in the hell does a fifteen year old needed to have sex for

anyway.

"I guess, but you know everyone is coming over. Kedra

and my dad." He let out a loud sigh because I knew that he didn't

want to give in, but he did.

Climbing on top of him, to thank him for everything, I

placed my hand on his neck. "You still love me?" David was

already ready because of held himself up so that I could easily

slide down on it.

"I'm going to always love you. You stood by me my

entire career with all the lies the media tried to put out, not

mention you are the mother of my kids. You nearly died giving

birth to the twins. You're my superhero." His words made me

work harder. I wanted to show him how grateful I was to have

him in my life.

****

Sunday had come sooner than expected, and once we got

home from church, everyone was ready to eat. Kedra, Helena,

and I were in the kitchen preparing dinner for the families. All the kids were in the movie room and the men were watching the game in the front. For a winter day, it was really beautiful outside, but nobody thought the idea of eating by the pool would be fun.

"Mom, he's down the street. How do I look?" Denise did a spin in her dress. She was radiant. Her skin was glowing and her hair was so cute in the big bun on top of her head.

"I told her she looked fine." Stephanie, Kedra's daughter, walked in the kitchen behind Denise.

"You look stunning." I placed my hand over my chest. The doorbell rung and that made me anxious too. When I spoke to Zyan's mother over the phone, I invited her to stay for dinner too.

Denise rushed into the bathroom off of the kitchen so that she could give herself one final look. I tried to make sure that the pasta I was making was ok before I walked away to meet our guests. Before I could make my way to the door, I heard my husband call some a female dog.

David never cursed so I became alarmed. I was confused because when I got to the door, I just saw a white woman and her biracial son. "Hannah, I swear this better be a different little boy because if this is him, I going to ring your neck."

I looked back at the boy who actually favored my husband and my son. From the jaw line to the way his chin came to a slight point. This boy had to be the boy that David signed off his rights to all those years ago. My husband was fuming, still going off. After a while, the boy became defensive over his mother and sized my husband up.

"Oh my gosh! Dad, no! Don't embarrass me." Denise was panicking, running over to split up her farther and his long-lost son.

"Denise, back the hell up and you and him stay in a child's place. Tell him that I'm his farther, Hannah. Tell him that you played me into signing over my rights. There was never an adoption huh? You realized I didn't want anything to do with your trailer park behind so you made me miss out on my son's life!"

By now, everyone was standing in my foyer trying to see. Hannah was crying. She looked over at her son, reaching out her hand. "No, is this true? Is he my farther? You said he was dead. Ma, he looks very much alive to me!"

"Zyan, look at me. I did what was best for you. He didn't want to be a family." She kept trying to pull him to closer to her, but he hit her hand away every time. Yea, he hit his mother's hand away.

Denise looked over at me, confused as if I had the answers. I knew some things, but I didn't know it all. Right now, I didn't have many answers to give. I knew that everyone needed to calm down so we could talk about everything. I also knew that there probably wouldn't be a family dinner tonight.

"Hannah, I swear to God!" David punched a hole in my wall. Demi started crying, running over to me. Daniel was just as lost as Denise, but my gangsta child, Dakota moved past her cousins to see everything.

"Morray, you want me to bring the kids back upstairs," Kedra asked me. I nodded my head at her, but I rubbed Demi's back before taking her hand and passing her over to her aunt. The men and Helena went back to the living room. Daniel went with Stephanie and her sister outside, so it was just the five of us standing here.

"Ma, tell me this man isn't my farther. Tell me you wouldn't lie to me like that." Zyan walked up on his mother. She backed herself in the corner then turned her head to look at me.

Now see Hannah was more wrong than right in this situation, but I knew everyone was entitled to make mistakes. I knew that I had made my fair share of them, but I've grown so much the past sixteen years and I was sure Hannah had as well.

"Babe, can we calm down? We can go in the dining room and talk. I'm sure Hannah has a perfectly good explanation for all of this." I placed my hand on his shoulder. David turned to look back at me and nodded his head.

I led the way to the dining room and took the seat to the right of the head of the table. David sat down as the head, Denise sat next to me, leaving Hannah and Zyan to sit across from us with Zyan sitting the closest to David.

Kayla Andrè

No one said anything for the first five minutes of us sitting there. David looked over at Hannah with hate in his eyes and tears resting in the corners of them. Denise and Zyan didn't want to make eye contact with each other and I was guessing it was because they were feeling like they'd committed incest. All of this reminded me of Kimora and David.

"So you are my dad?" Zyan broke the ice. David nodded his head to answer the question. Denise looked at me and grabbed my hand. "How were you able to give me up so easily?"

"It wasn't easy. I cried about that decision, but I thought I was doing what was best for you, but I guess I was wrong. I did it because I love you, and I know that sounds crazy, but it's true. At that time, I had so much going on that I wouldn't have been who you needed me to be.

I never once forgot about you. Matter of fact, every Christmas we buy you a gift and sit it under the tree. You will forever be my first born, and to be honest I know how you feel. I didn't find out who my real dad was until I was about nineteen.

He's actually sitting in that living room now, and we're close like we've been father and son my entire life.

I want to apologize because when I signed over my rights, I thought it was for you to have a better life. I was told that your mom and I both were giving you to a better family, but I guess the joke was on me because she made me give up my rights in order to keep you for herself. Crazy part is though, Hannah, I thought you wanted my baby because my family had money."

All eyes were now on Hannah who was trying to gather her words, but her tears wouldn't let her mouth open. Denise nudged me under the table to get my attention. "You never told me that Dad had a baby with a White woman," she whispered in my ear. I looked back over at her, shrugging my shoulders. I didn't know what difference it was going to make if I did tell her.

"Ma, say something. I need to know!"

"It wasn't that I didn't want David in your life, but I didn't have a choice. The day you were born and we found out you were a boy instead of the girl we had planned for, a man came into my room saying he had become on behalf of the Martin family.

He came in to tell me that the family didn't need any more boys and Zyan and I would both be killed if I were to contact you again. I was given three million dollars to leave you alone. The plan was for me to leave town, but once I saw you'd signed to the LA Dodgers, I decided there was no need.

I was wrong for having the woman lie to you, but in that moment, I thought my child was going to be killed. I loved him more than life itself, and I didn't want him to die. Zyan forgive me for doing that, but at the time I did what I thought was best."

Listening to her story, I believed every word. The Martins were some despicable people, and I knew for sure they were serious about killing her. I will never forget that they killed Liana. To this very day, she was still a missing person. That family had a very far reach.

After sitting around the table for almost an hour, Zyan and David had decided to come try and have a relationship. Hannah kept apologizing, but my daughter was my concern.

Zyan was her first love and to find out he was her brother was probably killing her on the inside. Once dinner was over, everyone was gone, and my house was clean, I decided to go up to her room.

She was sitting at her vanity, wrapping her hair, when I walked in. My heart was aching for my first born. "Baby, I'm here if you want to talk. I know this thing with Zyan is probably bothering you."

Denise sat her brush down on the table and turned to me. "Mommy, yes I did think that Zyan was nice, but I was just with him because he was as popular as I was. Daddy told me that I was *The Martin*. The only girl born in two generations! Zyan was never fit to run an empire with me. He would make a good addition to my team though. I was thinking Daniel, but Zyan is more muscular. He could be my enforcer like Uncle Troy. Daddy says I'm going to need a right-hand man. Daddy also says he doesn't know why you're with David. You could've been a queen, but now you're around here looking like *The Real Housewives of Tampa*. Daddy says you can always come home if you want." She flashed her perfectly white teeth and shrugged

her shoulders before turning around. "I love David because he's

my farther too, but do you ever miss Daddy? Daddy says he

misses you."

I watched her as she finished up her nightly routine, and

although I wanted to hop down her throat and remind her how

badly she had me twisted, I didn't. I wanted to sit down and

explain everything to her. From my first day teaching at Tampa

Bay to the divorce from her father. I even wanted to tell her about

the Senior flown her to Cuba and tried keeping her there so I

couldn't find her, but I couldn't. I had tried desperately to keep

my child pure and away from the negativity of the Martin family,

but somehow I knew that it was ineludible. She had just shown

me that it was in her DNA.

The End

For Updates and New Release, Follow Me Camera!

Facebook:

@Kayla André

Like Page:

Kayla's Reading Corner

Reading Group:

Story Time With Kayla